The Pirate Was Shockingly Authentic.

Dressed entirely in black, six feet tall, with terrific shoulders, the man was fascinating—there was no denying it. An ebony bandana didn't quite contain the thick abundance of glossy black hair.

He wore a single gold-loop earring, a short curving sword in a leather scabbard at his side and—Gabriella took one more look to be sure—an honest-to-goodness peg leg!

He looked real enough to have just stepped off the deck of a Spanish galley. The overall effect of his appearance was dramatic, astounding.

He was the most arrestingly gorgeous male she'd ever laid eyes on.

Although not conscious of moving, she suddenly found herself face-to-face with him. Her heartbeat drummed in her ears.

"Long John Silver?"

He held out one darkly tanned hand. His voice was soft and slightly hoarse, almost a caress. "Long John. At your service."

Dear Reader:

What makes a romance? A special man, of course, and Silhouette Desire is celebrating that fact with twelve of them! From June 1989 to May 1990 every month will spotlight an irresistible Silhouette Desire hero—our *Man of the Month*.

Created by your best-loved authors, you'll find these men utterly compelling. You'll be swept away by Diana Palmer's Mr June, (whom some of you may remember from his brief appearance in *Fit for a King)*, and Joan Hohl's Mr July is enough to make any woman's toes curl . . .

Don't let these men get away!

Please write to us:

Jane Nicholls
Silhouette Books
PO Box 236
Thornton Road
Croydon
Surrey
CR9 3RU

MARCY GRAY
A Pirate at Heart

Silhouette Desire

Originally Published by Silhouette Books
a division of
Harlequin Enterprises Ltd.

First published in Great Britain in 1989
by Silhouette Books, Eton House, 18-24 Paradise Road,
Richmond, Surrey TW9 1SR

© Marcy Gray 1989

Silhouette, Silhouette Desire and Colophon are
Trade Marks of Harlequin Enterprises B.V.

ISBN 0 373 57602 X

22—8907

Made and printed in Great Britain

MARCY GRAY

has always loved reading romances and can't resist a story that makes her cry. Though she has been writing romances for ten years, this is her first Silhouette Book. She looks for story ideas in everyday life and spends hours just watching people to help develop her characters. Her love of travel enables her to research her books.

One

Gabriella hated parties. Call it paranoia, but she always felt awkward in crowds, as if she were under inspection. That came, she figured in a moment of self-analysis, from years of trying to impress her regrettably snobbish parents.

Even though her parents had no connection whatsoever with this Halloween party to be hosted by the San Angelo, Texas, city council, she still didn't want to attend. With the Tulsa art show just a couple of months away and plenty of work left to be done on the Comanche chieftain, she would be better off locking herself in her studio until she had all her pieces ready for the foundry. The last thing she ought to do was spend an entire evening trying to persuade the city fathers to commission a bronze sculpture commemorating the area's history.

But her yearly tax notice had arrived in the morning mail, along with the electric bill and a statement announcing her woefully inadequate bank balance. Even if Gabriella gave up eating for six months, there wasn't going to be nearly enough money to pay the property taxes. According to the bank, she was exactly $92.37 away from bankruptcy.

"What are you going to do?" her friend Louise asked, worried by the way Gabriella had been standing at the studio door, staring out at the fields that hadn't been cultivated in the three years since her grandfather's death. "Will you ask your father to help?"

Gabriella forced herself to turn, to walk over to her worktable and sit down, propping her elbows on the scarred surface and clasping her hands together. "It wouldn't do any good to ask my father." She spoke with a calmness that belied the growing terror inside her. What *was* she going to do, dear God? If she didn't come up with a large sum of money, fast, she was going to lose her farm, her studio, her grandfather's home...everything she'd worked so hard to hang on to! Almost as bad as forfeiting the old man's legacy would be the stigma of failure, the admission that she just didn't have what it took.

"But have you tried asking?" Louise persisted.

Sighing, Gabriella ran a hand through the long, undisciplined thickness of her dark brown hair. "When I quit school and moved down here to try to make a living with my sculpture, my father told me I couldn't possibly succeed, that my talent wasn't anything special."

"He was wrong," Louise said. "You have a remarkable talent; everyone who sees your work says so."

"Thanks." Gabriella's warm smile transformed her face, lighting up her wide brown eyes and wrinkling her small but rather elegant nose. Almost at once she sobered again. "To entice me to come back to New York and finish college, Daddy offered me a huge advance on my trust fund—the one I'll get in two years, when I'm twenty-five. When I refused to do that, he cut off my allowance completely." She looked at her friend gravely. "The way things are going, I'll be lucky if I even *make* it to twenty-five. The taxes are due in January."

With a trace of anxiety Louise said, "But surely your father will lend you the money! After all, this land belonged to his own father; your dad grew up here. And according to everything I've heard, he's got millions."

A frown tugged at Gabriella's delicately arching brows. "I don't think you understand what I'm saying, Louise. My father really doesn't want me to be a sculptress. He thinks women—his women, at least—should look pretty and be taken care of, just like my mother. He thinks all I need is a husband...preferably, one who's listed in the Social Register. And if letting his own father's homestead be taken over for nonpayment of taxes will make me see the light and return to New York, then Daddy's willing to sit back and watch while the sheriff kicks me out of my home."

Louise shook her head, saddened by what she was hearing. "You really love this place, don't you?"

Tears blurred Gabriella's dark eyes, and she couldn't answer.

"All right, so we can count out your father's help," the small, freckled blonde said decisively. "I don't suppose you've still got any of the cash inheritance from your Grandfather Michaelson?"

Clearing her throat, Gabriella said, "I've been living off that so long, it's just about used up. In the past year I've only sold four of my bronze pieces."

"Times are hard. Believe me, if Jack and I weren't having so much trouble getting his engine repair business off the ground, we'd lend you the money. Even though we moved here to Bronte six months ago, nearly everyone in town still takes anything that needs fixing thirty miles to San Angelo for repairs rather than give Jack a chance to prove he's a great mechanic." An idea suddenly occurred to her. "You don't think it could be that we're not friendly enough, do you?"

Gabriella shook her head emphatically. She'd never met anyone more outgoing than the energetic young woman from Mississippi who'd struck up a conversation with Gabriella as they both waited in line at the grocery store. That had been five months ago, and Louise hadn't really stopped talking since. "I couldn't accept a loan from you anyway, Louise. You and Jack have already done more for me than I can ever repay." She thrust out her chin. "I have to make the money myself. I have to prove my father was wrong—I don't need a man to take care of me."

Louise jumped up and hugged her. "Atta girl! You're going to get the sculpture commission from the San Angelo city council, aren't you?"

If only it were as easy as Louise made it sound! "I'm darn sure going to try," Gabriella said grimly.

"We already know they love your work. No other artist even has a chance at the commission."

Gabriella nodded; one of the city councilmen had indeed assured her that she was the first choice...*if* the council voted to authorize the sculpture. But that was a very big if, thanks to an outspoken newspaper editor named J. C. Lindsey, who apparently had a personal grudge against art. Mr. Lindsey had been running editorials in the local paper for months, urging the reallocation of the funds for something other than a sculpture.

"All you have to do," Louise continued confidently, "is show up at the party and use some of your Eastern finishing school charm on these good ol' boys on the city council. That cantankerous Mr. Lindsey with his poison-pen editorials won't stand a chance against you. Just wait'll you see the outfit I made for you to wear. You'll knock 'em dead!''

The moment Gabriella tried on the midcalf length ballerina dress made from frothy pink netting with a low-cut satin bodice that gave her skin a golden luster, a peculiar excitement sprang to life inside her. The dress made her feel one hundred percent female and totally beautiful.

She stood in front of the long mirror that hung outside the bathroom door and scrutinized herself from every angle. "I don't know, Louise. It's a fantastic dress. Thank you for making it. The thing is . . . I'm just not sure it's *me*."

"That's the beauty of it: this is a costume party. You're not supposed to go as Gabriella Michaelson, sculptress. Besides, the dress is perfect for you! You're an absolute vision in it." Louise watched her friend in smug delight. "I knew you would be."

Gabriella forced a smile that disguised her lingering fear. "Don't get carried away, hmm? I haven't got that commission yet, and I'm not so sure going to this party looking like a Barbie doll is the way to get it."

"But you *will* go, won't you?"

Pivoting, she studied her reflection. The lovely creature who looked back at her was someone she didn't really know. One reason she'd been glad to leave Barnard College and New York City behind was to escape the constant need to dress up and socialize.

But it wasn't as if she had much choice at this point. Her only hope of saving her home was to go to the party and charm everyone in sight. Gabriella's eyes began to glitter at the prospect of meeting her opposition. "Yes, I'll go."

She couldn't resist one more quick pirouette before slipping out of the dress. The skirt rustled seductively against her long legs and the satin hugged her curves, and Gabriella shivered in anticipation. She just might enjoy this party after all.

Christian went to Big Spring on business early Saturday morning and didn't get back to San Angelo until after dark. He was so hungry and tired, he almost settled for grabbing a sandwich and bed. But this was Halloween, the night of the city council costume party. He had no intention of missing that affair, even if he fell asleep in the middle of it.

After showering and getting ready, he took a couple of apples from the refrigerator and ate one as he drove toward the Cactus Hotel. Just after he turned onto Oakes Street, he passed a small, hunched-over figure hobbling past the darkened businesses, lugging a brown shopping bag with handles, and he swore beneath his breath when the faint streetlight revealed the old woman's bare arms. He recognized Tilly Mitchell—"Silly Tilly" as the local kids had called her for all of Christians' thirty years. Damn, the weather was already turning cold and the wind was picking up. She was going to freeze without a coat.

He swung his Jaguar around in a sharp U-turn and slid to a stop along the curb. Forgetting the way he was dressed, he climbed out of the low-slung car to approach the shuffling form with an offer of a ride.

Tilly took one look at Christian and let out a scream of mortal terror, then grabbed a baseball bat that protruded from her bag and began thrashing it in his direction.

One arm raised to ward off the wild blows, Christian retreated hastily. From a safe distance he jerked off the black bandanna that had covered his equally-dark hair and wished he didn't have a lethal-looking cutlass dangling from his belt. He suppressed a chuckle at the picture he knew he must make—like a character right out of *Treasure Island* with his old-fashioned peg leg. "Miss Mitchell, it's me—John

Christian. I'm on my way to a Halloween party. I'm supposed to be a pirate."

She peered at him through the dimness. "John Christian?" Her voice quavered uncertainly. Teetering a couple of steps closer, she stared first at his sword, then at his face and finally at his leg, bending down a bit to get a better look. Satisfied that he was really who he said he was, she straightened and shook her finger at him. "You scared the life out of me, young man!"

Christian knew better than to laugh out loud. "Sorry," he said. "I just stopped to give you a ride. It's too cold for you to be walking."

"Fiddlesticks! I'm taking my daily constitutional. Fresh air is good for a body."

From the looks of her, she'd had plenty of fresh air lately, and very few amenities like bed and bath. He suspected Tilly was living on the streets, and the idea bothered him. Winter was coming, and Tilly must be pushing seventy. Her sister had died last spring, and Christian seemed to recall hearing something about the family home having been sold to pay debts.

He flashed her a shamelessly charming smile as he took the shopping bag out of her hands. "Well, Miss Mitchell, I'm glad to hear you believe in staying in shape, but I imagine you've had enough exercise for one day." As he talked, he steered her by the elbow over to his car. "Where have you been staying lately?"

"Here and there," Tilly said vaguely, letting him help her settle into the seat. "Around."

"I see." Christian groped for tact as he got inside and put the car in gear. "How about if I take you to see Mr. Schultz at the Methodist Church and let him arrange a place for you to stay tonight?"

"Mr. Schultz? Your daddy's not the pastor there?"

"Not anymore." Not in over ten years, he might have reminded her. He offered her the remaining apple, and she took it so eagerly that he wondered when she'd last eaten.

"I dunno, John Christian," she said between bites. "If it was your daddy, I wouldn't mind..."

"Mr. Schultz is nice, too. You'll like him."

Tilly finished the apple in record time, tossed the core out the window and wiped the juice from her hands onto her grubby-looking dress. "If you say so." She glanced around at the interior of his car, apparently having lost interest in where he was taking her. "Goodness me, John Christian— this is nice! Is it new?"

"No, ma'am. I've had this car thirteen years."

Already off on another track, she mumbled, "You turned out all right after all. Sure surprised some folks."

Christian didn't pursue the conversation with Tilly. When he had escorted her up to the parsonage door and handed her over to Philip Schultz's capable wife, the old woman surprised him by reaching up to pat his cheek. "You're a fine boy, John Christian. Too handsome for your own good. Used to be a devil, but you turned out right." She turned away with a cackling laugh. "Make a pretty fair pirate, you do. Run along now and capture some girl!"

Disregarding the cold, Christian rolled down both windows when he got back in the car to air out the interior. The leather seats in his lovingly restored 1968 Jaguar were soft and porous, and they tended to absorb the scents of his passengers. It had been quite a while, he figured ruefully, since Tilly had bathed.

His mouth quirked. Tilly treated him as if he were a slightly larger version of the teenage hell-on-wheels she remembered. And she had no home, no place to sleep, not enough to eat. He knew from experience that hunger wasn't something to be laughed at. Tilly was the reason he was going to the party tonight.

He arrived after the party was in full swing, with a live band and dancing at one end of the room and a buffet at the other. Thankfully the hotel ballroom was big enough that he could stand back and get a clear view of the crowd. If he intended to accomplish anything this evening, he needed to locate Gabriella Michaelson and size her up.

A couple of minutes later, Christian easily picked out the sculptress among a group of admirers, holding a drink in one hand and doing a lot more listening than talking. Watching her, he felt a peculiar spiral of warmth uncurl in his stomach and spread all the way through him. Mmm, this might be interesting.

Gabriella guessed that the pirate hadn't been there very long when she noticed him. In a virtual sea of white sheeted ghosts and green faced goblins, the realism of his costume was as conspicuous as a flashing neon sign. Early in the evening she'd met a rather interesting ear of corn who proved to be a Methodist minister in disguise. After talking to him awhile she'd been disappointed to learn that he sided with the opposition. In his tactfully-stated opinion, San Angelo needed a shelter for the homeless far more than it needed a new sculpture. From the sad tales he told her, she understood where he got that idea and didn't try to change his mind.

Most of those who hovered around Gabriella expressed a liking for her talent, even though the only piece of her work any of them had ever seen was the tabletop edition of the buffalo currently on exhibit at the library. Except for the minister, nobody would admit to having the slightest idea why she shouldn't get the commission. After priming herself all week, Gabriella was deflated to realize that the newspaper editor hadn't bothered coming forward to meet her. It made the evening seem rather pointless.

Small wonder, then, that her straying attention was snagged by that shockingly authentic pirate. He moved through the crowd slowly, pausing to speak to a person here or there but always within sight of Gabriella. She even got the feeling that he was edging toward her—that he was as aware of her as she was of him—and the possibility sent a delicious tingle down her spine.

She finally put aside her margarita and stared without shame. Dressed entirely in black, six feet tall with terrific shoulders and not an ounce of fat, the man was fascinating—there was no denying it. An ebony bandanna didn't quite contain the thick abundance of his glossy blue-black hair. He wore a single gold-loop earring, a short curving sword in a leather scabbard at his side and—Gabriella took one more look to be sure—an honest-to-goodness peg leg!

The overall effect of his appearance was dramatic, astounding. He looked real enough to have just stepped off the deck of a Spanish galleon. Peg leg and all, he was the most arrestingly good-looking male she'd ever laid eyes on.

Oblivious to the conversation around her, she watched him come closer. When he smiled at another woman, a stab of some unidentifiable emotion sliced through Gabriella, intense and highly disturbing. When he half-turned and his eyes met hers and held without looking away, she felt as if the very breath were being sucked out of her lungs.

Although not conscious of moving, Gabriella suddenly found herself face-to-face with the pirate, her heartbeat drumming in her ears. His eyes, she discovered, were hazel—golden brown flecked with green. They were also warm with something like approval.

Christian gazed at the enchanting young woman in the pink ballerina dress and swallowed the knot of pleasure that formed in his throat. *Gabriella Michaelson,* he thought with an inner groan. He hadn't expected this. Oh, he'd seen her picture, so her beauty came as no surprise. But he hadn't known how unsettling it would be just to look at her in a crowd. And to stand this close—he could feel himself sinking into the lush velvet darkness of her eyes. He had a strong urge to run an experimental finger down the glowing softness of her cheek, to make sure she was real, but he didn't dare touch her like that. The lady would think he was crazy.

The lady thought he was *gorgeous.* Knowing better than to tell him that, she looked him in the eye and said the only other thing that came to mind. "Long John Silver?"

His remarkable eyes blinked in momentary surprise, narrowed briefly and then crinkled at the corners when amusement rearranged his features into an unembarrassed smile. "Oh. Yes. Right." He held out one dark-skinned hand. "Long John at your service."

His voice was almost a caress, soft and slightly hoarse. Her hand was swallowed up by the pliant warmth of his, and she thought her knees would give way when a hot melting sensation raced from her fingertips to her toes.

Gabriella drew back her hand reluctantly, determined to keep him talking. "I do admire your costume, Long John. But I don't think anyone expected you to carry it quite that far!"

He fingered the gold earring. "You mean this? It's left over from my rebellious youth. I haven't worn an earring since I was seventeen."

"I wasn't referring to your earring," she said dryly.

The sparks of humor in his eyes told her he knew very well what she was referring to. "Actually, my leg is another souvenir of the wild oats I sowed as a teenager."

Gabriella looked up at him curiously. She'd never met anyone like this intriguing pirate. "That brings to mind motorcycles and street-gang fights."

"Try motorcycles and telephone poles, colliding at high speed."

She winced. "I'll bet you were a trial to your parents."

He nodded, thinking that he'd never seen such long, thick eyelashes or such eyes. Her hair was done up in some kind of fancy braid on the back of her head, and his fingers itched to take it down, to tangle into the silky dark strands. He could picture it lying tousled and soft on the gold-tinted skin of her shoulders and tumbling down her slim straight back. He could just imagine sifting the incredible texture through his fingers.

Christian spoke without planning to. "Miss Michaelson—Gabriella?—let's get out of here."

When her eyes widened in astonishment and he realized what he'd said, he wondered if he could have flipped, to harbor such ideas about Gabriella Michaelson. But he looked at her again and knew in a blinding flash that all his thoughts about this woman were divinely inspired.

"Lets...what?" she asked, so taken aback by his request that she forgot her question about how he knew her name. She looked as if she doubted his sanity, too.

He bent his head closer to be sure no one else overheard, and his subtly sexy fragrance engulfed her. "Go for a drive. Talk. Get something to eat. I'm starved!"

She really shouldn't leave the party. She ought to stay until the band went home just to be sure she didn't miss a chance to argue her cause. But it had to be after ten o'clock already. If Mr. Lindsey was going to throw down the gauntlet, he should have done so before now.

When Gabriella lifted her chin and smiled at him, Christian knew she was going to say yes, and the tightness in his chest loosened. Suddenly he could breathe again, which made him realize just how terrified he'd been that she would refuse. He smiled back and took her arm, anxious to get her out before anything foiled this escape.

As they threaded their way toward the exit, she purposely lagged a step behind him. When he looked back at her inquiringly, she said, "Shouldn't you tell me your name?"

His smile widened, showing off his white teeth and rakish charm. "I thought you were going to call me Long John."

Just then, a woman passing them said, "You're not kidnapping our sculptress, are you, John Christian?"

When her handsome pirate put his forefinger to his lips and swore the lady to silence, Gabriella stopped dragging her heels and went with him willingly.

"So you really *are* Long John, hmm?" she teased him, watching him steal her right out of the midst of the crowd with all the skill of a cat burglar. "Long John Christian?" He flashed her a sidelong grin acknowledging it.

In no time, he had her out of the building and down the street and was handing her into a sleek red sports car, then unfastening the cutlass from his belt and dropping it behind the front seat. The peg leg, she observed as he got in and started the engine, didn't seem to slow him down very much.

When he stopped a block later for a red light, he let out a shaky breath and glanced over at her. The unexpectedness of this situation had him feeling somewhat stunned, but undeniably exuberant. He was going to have to be very careful how he handled things tonight. There was more at stake than he'd first anticipated.

His blood pulsed with excitement at the sight of Gabriella just inches away in the intimate dimness of his car, pervading the small compartment with her delicious scent. Still fighting the urge to take down her hair, he allowed himself instead to brush a fingertip along her bare shoulder.

He felt her shiver at his touch. "It's a little late to be asking," he said huskily, "but did you have a wrap?"

Gabriella dragged her thoughts away from him and considered his question, then shook her head in sudden dismay. No, she hadn't worn a coat, but she *had* ridden over from home tonight with Louise and Jack Grissom.

"The friends I came with are going to kill me," she said. "When it comes time to take me home, they won't have any idea where I disappeared to."

As the light turned green, he took his foot off the brake and sent her another of his irresistible grins. "They can't very well kill you if they can't find you. And *I'm* taking you home tonight." He didn't intend to share her with anyone else.

She liked his reasoning. Settling down onto the comfortable leather seat, she said, "Okay, but get ready for a long drive. I live near Bronte."

"I think my car can make it that far. You're not in a hurry, though, are you? There isn't anyone waiting up for you at home?" To his relief, she shook her head and informed him that she lived alone.

As he drove, he reached up and tugged the bandanna off his head, tossing it into the back seat and running his fingers through his thick black hair in a futile attempt to smooth it down. It looked rumpled and inviting to Gabriella, who clasped her hands together on her lap to stop herself from combing it for him.

Still keeping one hand on the steering wheel, he unhooked the gold earring and put it in the glove box. As he reached across her, his arm disturbed the whispery pink netting of her skirt, and she felt her heart stop for just a moment before his hand returned harmlessly to driving.

She gulped. "Where are we going?"

"Someplace quiet for a good steak," he said, glancing sideways at her. "If you don't object to the way I'm dressed."

"What's wrong with the way you're dressed?"

Was she serious? He couldn't tell. "Well...you may find this hard to believe, but I usually look fairly...shall we say *normal*? If you like, I can run by my place and change."

She suddenly realized he was talking about his leg. In the space of a few minutes, Gabriella had forgotten all about that. She wanted to show him that it didn't matter. Besides, the undercurrent of sexual tension darting back and forth between them warned her that it would be a mistake for her to go anywhere near his home. There was no telling what might happen if she did.

She managed a casual grin. "Why don't we just go eat? You're about to find out what an expensive date I can be. I feel as if I haven't eaten in a month." She didn't mention that with her financial troubles, it might be her last good meal for a long time.

Christian relaxed. Although he'd walked into manhood minus half of his left leg and was no longer unduly sensitive about it, still there was always a difficult moment upon meeting a new lady when he wondered how she would react to his handicap. This lady, he was glad to note, seemed to take it in stride.

"Let's feed you, then Miss Michaelson," he said, his smile doing strange things to her equilibrium.

They had almost reached Zentner's when she muttered half to herself, "I didn't really expect to be enjoying this evening so much." Christian arched a dark, quizzical eyebrow at her. "I should have stuck it out at the party. Five minutes after I left, the jerk probably showed up to cram his opinion down everyone's throats.''

"The...who?" But with a sinking feeling in the pit of his stomach, he thought he knew exactly what jerk she was talking about.

Two

———

Gabriella didn't bother hiding her disgust. "The self-righteous editor of the *San Angelo Journal*. Mr. J. C. Lindsey. He'll probably run a scathing editorial in tomorrow's paper, claiming that I left the party early because I was afraid to face him. The rat."

No one had ever accused Christian of not having a sense of humor. If he'd been holding this discussion with any other person, he might have laughed at the critic's perception of J. C. Lindsey. But with Gabriella being the critic, it wasn't very funny. He wondered if there was a way out of this mess. "You think he'd do that?" he asked after a moment.

Her voice was low and tight. "I wouldn't put anything past that snake in the grass."

He cleared his throat. "He's the enemy?"

She looked at him as if he must be feebleminded. "Didn't you read the column he wrote last week about my sculpture?"

"Well, uh, yes, as a matter of fact, I did." He turned into the restaurant's parking lot and found a space for the Jag. After killing the motor, he made no move to get out. "But it seemed to me that the editorial focused on San Angelo's serious economic needs rather than the merit of your sculpture."

"According to him, my sculpture *has* no merit."

The hurt beneath her flippant tone evoked his compassion. He'd never said anything like that, and it bothered him that she thought he had.

He slid his arm behind her and cupped his warm palm against the back of her neck, just beneath the feathery curls that had escaped from her french braid. "Gabriella," he said with a tenderness that was wholly unexpected and infinitely precious to her ears, "that's not true. Nobody who has seen your work could possibly doubt your talent."

As he spoke he stroked his thumb lightly along her skin, soothing her, deliberately seeking to replace her anger with a more pleasurable sensation.

"Thanks." The single word was hushed, shaky. A potent heat had begun sizzling through her veins, and she shut her eyes and tried to ignore it. "You don't seem to know this Lindsey creep, though."

Christian asked wryly, "Do *you* know him?"

"Not personally, thank heaven."

"Well...maybe it would be a good idea for you to meet him." He was still working the slow, easy magic on her with his fingertips. "You could help him see your side, and maybe you'd come to understand why he feels the way he does."

Gabriella felt herself sinking lower in the bucket seat, as though she were dissolving from his touch. "I already know why he feels that way. Because he's an uncivilized boor." She tilted her nose in the air and quoted with delicate disdain, "'Art has no enemy except ignorance.'"

When Christian withdrew his hand to cover his sudden bout of coughing, Gabriella sat up a little reluctantly. "Sorry. I tend to get carried away on the subject of Mr. Lindsey and his journalistic dictatorship. Bring on the steak and I promise not to mention him again."

By now Christian was having second thoughts about taking Gabriella to a popular place like Zentner's. He was known there. What were the chances they would get through dinner without someone calling him by name? By his *full* name, that is. He considered turning to her before they even got out of the car and saying, "By the way, Miss Michaelson, *I'm* John Christian Lindsey."

Imagining her response to that, he flinched. No, he had better lay a lot more groundwork before he told her the truth.

He leaned back in the seat and raked his hand through his hair in a gesture of weariness that wasn't entirely feigned. "Gabriella, would you mind if we went somewhere else? Someplace not so crowded."

He didn't give a reason, mainly because he couldn't think of a plausible one. Sneaking a look at him, Gabriella told him nonchalantly that it didn't matter to her where they ate. On the off-chance that her bold pirate was actually more self-conscious than she'd thought at first, she informed him that there was a place just up the street that she frequented whenever she was in town shopping, a place that made superb hamburgers and even had a drive-through window. She didn't mention its chief attraction for her—that it had the cheapest food in San Angelo.

"I usually just eat in the car," she said with studied innocence.

Christian wasn't sure he believed her, but he was in no position to argue. If they picked up some food and took it to his house to eat, she would be sure to see his diplomas or the framed journalism awards on his walls.

The hamburgers really were good. Gabriella laughed at Christian because he wore such a skeptical expression at first and then ended up driving back through the line twice to order additional burgers and fries. "Where are you putting all that food?" she asked, appraising his lean hard length with awe. "You must have a hollow leg."

"I do. It's at home."

He kept his face perfectly straight until she clamped a hand over her mouth in chagrin, and then he tossed back his head and laughed. "Really, Gabriella, you left yourself wide open for that one."

"I guess I did." She giggled sheepishly. "Sorry."

"Don't apologize. I've found it's best not to take my problems too seriously." He took a swig of his soft drink and then set it back on the console between them.

She watched him, thinking that there was something very open and easy about this man. The way he joked about his leg—the very fact that he went to the party as Long John Silver in the first place—testified to both his unpretentious honesty and his self-confidence. He was fun to be around. And she, who had never completely let down her guard with anyone, felt instinctively that she could trust him. He'd even managed to get her mind off her own problems for an hour or two.

It didn't take Christian long to figure out that sharing hamburgers with Gabriella in the cozy warmth of his car was far better than dining at the Ritz with anyone else. He couldn't remember when he'd enjoyed an evening, or someone's company, this much.

He thought she looked like a vision in pink against the red leather upholstery. When she caught him staring at her appreciatively, she stretched with an almost feline grace and then settled back against the door and proceeded to stare at *him*. The good bone structure of his face and his dark, compactly muscled attractiveness made her want to touch him, to explore his shape.

"I'd like to do a sculpture of you sometime," she announced. Before he had time to do more than blink in surprise, she said, "Where were you born?"

He gathered up the remains of their meal and stuffed it into two paper bags. "Muleshoe. It's a little place in the Texas Panhandle."

He got out of the car and took the trash over to the nearest litter barrel, pausing to grin and wave at the youths who called out to him from another parked car. Gabriella didn't hear what they said to him, but she guessed it was a humorous reference to his peg leg.

When he climbed back inside, she picked up the topic where he'd left off. "I know where Muleshoe is. I just never would have figured it to be the home of Long John Christian."

He put on a thick Texas twang. "Cain't see me on a horse, huh?" When she laughed in delight, he reverted to his usual soft drawl. "And you... you originated in Manhattan, I believe."

"How did you guess? My accent?"

He merely smiled at that. She spoke with a pure enunciation that completely lacked any dialectal distinction, no doubt drilled into her at the Chapin School or Miss Porter's. Gabriella Michaelson was upper-class all the way.

Cocking his head, he studied her. "You went to Barnard a couple of years, majoring in... French literature, wasn't it?"

"Are you psychic? What else can you tell about me?"

Narrowing his eyes, he searched her face as if hunting for clues to her background, while in reality he was simply treating himself to the pleasure of looking at her.

After a couple of minutes, she began to fidget beneath his lazy scrutiny. "Come on, Long John. It shouldn't take you all night to figure out that I'm a Leo."

"Okay, okay. I'm working on it. How's this: You spent every penny of your allowance from the time you were ten years old on art lessons. The greatest influence on your sculpting was a teacher named Wilfred March, who introduced you to the lost-wax method. Three months after your first solo show in New York City, you moved to Bronte to work, and you've been participating in shows and selling regularly ever since."

Gabriella lifted one eyebrow. "You saw that in my face?"

"Was it accurate?"

"Except for that part about selling regularly. I haven't exactly been overwhelmed by the demand for my pieces." She almost added that this was why she needed the San Angelo commission so badly, but pride kept her from mentioning the disastrous state of her financial affairs.

She forced herself to speak lightly. "Okay, be honest, now. You didn't really get that from just looking at me, did you?"

Christian recognized and wondered about her deliberate subject change. He rubbed his jaw and answered absently. "No, I read that in your bio."

"And you remembered it? I'm impressed."

"Well, it hasn't been too long ago. You had that showing in Dallas, remember? I was there on business and stopped by to see it. I sent a friend back later to pick up one of your pieces for me."

The radiant pleasure that suffused her face made him glad he'd told her that, even if he was talking too much, getting close to dangerous territory.

"You did? Which one did you buy?"

"Palomino"

She stared at him with huge dark eyes. "Why did you want that one in particular?"

He shifted one shoulder. "I don't know. It affects me— the fluid lines, the strength of it. I think it's the best thing you've ever done."

"So do I!" She smiled as though he'd just given her a special gift. "It's my favorite, too."

He turned to face the windshield and wrapped the long fingers of both hands around the steering wheel. "Gabriella, would you do me a favor? Would you let me see your studio?"

She had no qualms about agreeing.

The headlights of the Jaguar swept into the driveway of a comfortable red-brick home that had been built, Christian estimated, soon after World War II. Gabriella directed him to park at the rear, near a garage that sheltered a classic 1955 Chevrolet.

"My grandfather bought that car new," she said when she saw his interest.

On the drive from San Angelo she'd given him a brief and carefully edited version of how twelve years earlier Eli Michaelson had converted the big storage room attached to his garage into a sculpting studio to entice his only granddaughter into spending her summers with him. Gabriella had never confided in anyone that she got little encouragement in her art from her father, who considered artists immoral, Bohemian and stuck somewhere at the very bottom of the social ladder. Still, her grandfather had intuitively perceived how his son, Andrew, stifled Gabriella's creative urges, attempting to mold her into a future perfect young debutante who would guarantee that the Michaelsons had really arrived in New York society.

In an effort to counter that repression, Eli had willed everything he had to her. Andrew certainly didn't need the inheritance; he'd made his first million manufacturing sports shoes before he was twenty-five years old, and he'd married well besides. But when Eli left Gabriella a studio, Andrew effectively tied her hands by taking away her allowance. The cost of living, the expense of working in bronze and the slump in the Texas economy and the market for art had done the rest. Three years after Eli's death, she was a hair's breadth away from calling it quits at the ripe old age of twenty-three.

Gabriella didn't reveal all those facts to John Christian. She kept things light as she told him about her childhood visits to Bronte, barely mentioning the years since she'd moved here.

As they got out of the car, Christian glanced back and said, "Nice house."

She murmured, "Yes, it is," and led the way across the driveway to the studio.

The night air was cold, and her teeth were chattering by the time she found the key beneath a brick in the flower bed and unlocked the door. Christian watched her, wondering again about her financial situation. A house like that plus five hundred acres of rich farmland must be worth quite a bit. And her father was an industrial giant, a local boy who'd made good on the East Coast.

Inside, she switched on the light and stood by the door, rubbing her bare arms to warm them up, while he wandered around looking at things.

He was surprised to find that her place of work, in addition to the expected worktables and supply storage cabinets and shelves of artwork, featured an old-fashioned brass bed and chest of drawers in one corner, a small kitchen area in another. The room was heated by a wood-burning stove that still put off an inviting warmth from an earlier fire. There was a scattering of clothes on the bed that both puzzled and intrigued him. It looked as if she'd gotten ready for the party right here.

Christian tried to push aside thoughts of Gabriella in a silken teddy, standing before that mirror and brushing her hair. He had come here to learn more about her work and, heaven help him, to talk to her about his role in the sculpture controversy. He was not here to fantasize about undressing her.

With an effort to act casual, he walked over to the shelves to look over the pieces, whose stages of development varied from crude lumps of paraffin wax to finished bronze. The completed pieces all had an attention to fine detail that fascinated him. Christian thought he could probably pick out her work from among anyone else's; somehow when he studied Gabriella's creations, his imagination soared.

But now he found his attention wandering to the artist herself as she ran a coffeepot full of water, then put it on the stove to heat. She was slim and supple, and she moved with the grace of a ballerina, a grace that her work reflected. Her golden skin and dark hair seemed all the richer by their contrast with that frothy pink dress.

When the coffee was done, Gabriella filled two mugs and carried them to the worktable, then hesitantly interrupted her guest's apparent absorption in her sculpture. "Would you like to sit down? I'm sorry I don't have a sofa or a comfortable chair to offer you."

He turned. "That stool will be fine. You've almost got this place fixed up like home as it is."

Amused, she realized he hadn't figured out that her studio *was* home. The fine brick house was closed up tight. Gabriella didn't need much room and couldn't afford to squander money on big utility bills. She'd even tried to rent out the place, but found no takers, what with people losing jobs and moving away.

She watched him sit down and stretch out his left leg under the table as if relieved to get his weight off of it. "That thing doesn't look very comfortable," she observed.

"It's not. Thanks to modern technology, I only have to wear it one night a year." At her puzzled look he said, "Halloween."

He lifted the cup, sniffed the aromatic steam and decided the coffee was too hot to drink. Setting it back down, he ordered himself to quit stalling. He rubbed his flattened hand over the battered surface of the table and then let his gaze drift around the room once more before meeting her eyes. "I never realized an artist's studio would be so much like..." He stopped himself from saying *like a newspaper office* and hesitated a moment, searching for a way to put it. Finally he grinned with disarming candor. "Well, so cluttered. I guess I didn't see the hard work that goes into creating, although Lord knows I should have. That Comanche figure is remarkable. If I weren't already a fan of yours, I would be after seeing it."

His words sounded like a compliment, but she read a tension in his facial muscles that she associated with bad news. She waited silently for him to go on.

"I think if anyone could create a fitting monument to San Angelo's history, you could. I've seen the proposal you submitted to the committee. It was outstanding." He stopped and looked away a moment before his gaze—warm, hazel and troubled—settled once more on her face. "The ones who object to the city commissioning you to do a sculpture aren't questioning your ability to do a good job. At this point, they would probably vote against Michelangelo."

She tightened her grip on the warm cup. "They've probably never even *heard* of Michelangelo."

His lips curved into a brief smile. "Gabriella, it's not simply a matter of a bunch of country hicks having no appreciation for culture. The problem here is an economic one."

"Well, at least Mr. Lindsey has convinced *you* of that."

Christian sighed, propped one elbow on the table and his chin on his hand and gazed at her levelly. "But it's true. More than half the oil wells in the area have shut down production and put thousands of people out of work. Farmers are being driven into bankruptcy by years of weather-related crop failures and poor prices for cattle and agricultural products. The depression of those two industries alone has dealt San Angelo a devastating blow, but it's bad all over Texas. Banks are failing right and left. Tax revenues are down. Unemployment is at an all-time high."

Gabriella squirmed uncomfortably, as her thoughts had just been down that same path. "I read the newspaper, Long John, even if I don't swallow its editorial policy verbatim. I know from firsthand experience that times are hard. But I also know the money for the sculpture is there. The funds were donated to honor the pioneers who settled the area, and if the money isn't utilized in the next three months, it'll revert to the estate of the family who left it to the city. I read *that* in the newspaper, too, as a matter of fact. So why doesn't that blasted editor stop stirring up trouble and let the city council get on with it?''

He started to question her about what she'd said—that she knew firsthand that times were hard—but then he decided she'd probably been speaking in generalizations. With her wealthy background, she couldn't possibly be short of money. Patiently he said, ''I don't think anyone can ignore the fact that what this community really needs now is more services to the poor and unemployed.''

Much as she would like to, she couldn't argue with him about that. But, it just wasn't fair; she was poor and all but unemployed, herself. ''But . . . the money was meant to be used for art. How can they just . . . just disregard the donor's specific intentions?''

''The farsighted donor included an option which allows the city council to reallocate the funds if they believe there's a more pressing need. And providing shelter for the homeless is very definitely a more pressing need, wouldn't you agree?''

Gabriella sat in aching silence, her throat constricted with despair. For the moment, all she could think about was that very soon she would be homeless, too. If she didn't get that commission—and she suddenly knew she wouldn't—she couldn't even afford to keep the electricity on another month, much less continue to sculpt or pay the taxes.

Still speaking gently, he said, ''Please don't think I'm discounting the importance of art, Gabriella. But it's hard for a man to appreciate culture if he hasn't eaten in two days...if he has no place to sleep and no way to support his family. That's what concerns your so-called opposition. They don't oppose art. They just feel it's more important to open a temporary shelter for people who would otherwise have to sleep on park benches and under railroad bridges.''

Crossing her forearms on the table, she leaned on them and stared past him as she brooded over his words. In spite of her certainty that the loss of this commission would herald the end of her sculpting career, she couldn't help being moved by his eloquence. What he said made sense. It also had a familiar ring to it—the ring of truth, she thought with a deep sigh.

Christian's low voice broke into her thoughts. "It's unsettling to see people I've known half my life suddenly reduced to living on the street, Gabriella." She turned to look at him. "Tonight I saw a lady out there who is old enough to be my grandmother. And there are children—little children." The intensity of his feelings shaded his eyes more green than gold. He reached for one of her hands, lacing their fingers together, and the seemingly unconscious gesture made her heart pound so hard she could barely hear his next words. "I just think we need to get our priorities straight. People have to matter more than things, Gaby— even culture—or we're in big trouble."

She knew she was a goner. Thanks to her persuasive pirate, she would never again feel right striving for the sculpture commission that she needed to salvage her own life.

And despite the fact that her troubles were growing by the day, the husky way he spoke her name—*Gaby*—did the most unbelievable things to her pulse rate.

He saw the look come into her eyes, the slow surrendering to a feeling too powerful to ignore, and then he felt the last of her resistence vanish as she returned his grip with delicate strength. She smiled, and his heart turned over a couple of times at the bittersweet warmth of that smile, at the shy yearning in her velvet brown eyes.

Keeping hold of her hand, he stood up to circle the table. On the other side, he pulled her to her feet and into his arms, and she came without hesitation. The tall dark pirate en-

folded his lady in a silent embrace, keeping a tight rein on
the hunger exploding inside him. When she lifted her face,
he covered her mouth in a kiss so tenderly provocative that
she melted against his hard length, wanting the fragile en-
chantment of this moment to go on forever. Wanting to
block out the future.

He slid one strong hand down her spine and drew her even
closer to him. He furrowed the other into her neat french
braid, tugging at hairpins wherever he found them, dropping them onto the floor, freeing her long hair so he could
see it, touch it all.

Just as it came loose and spilled in a raven wave down her
back, smothering his arm in silk, the studio door burst open
and a male voice snapped, ''Okay, buster, freeze! You move
an inch and you're dead meat!''

Three

Already racing, Gabriella's pulse rate skyrocketed at the interruption. She felt Long John's abrupt stillness, and a terrifying ten seconds passed before she realized she knew that voice.

Her fear receding, she turned to face the big man in the doorway. He wore a silver-sequined cowboy outfit and a white Stetson, and he was pointing a gun at her pirate.

"For Pete's sake, Jack Grissom, put down that BB pistol and quit acting like a fugitive from some television cop show! You're not even dressed for the part." When her best friend's husband lowered the gun sheepishly, she added, "What on earth has come over you?"

Jack's mouth dropped open. "What's come over me? You disappear from the party without saying a word to us, and then somebody tells us they saw you leave with this guy." He nodded at Long John. "We figured you'd been kidnapped."

"Kidnapped!" she exclaimed, feeling Christian's arm tighten around her waist. Just then Louise peeked in the door and, deciding it was safe, came inside. She had made matching Western costumes for Jack and herself, and Gabriella had jokingly told the couple when they picked her up that they looked like Roy Rogers and Dale Evans. Now she appealed to the elfin blonde. "Louise, has your husband flipped his lid? Why would he think I'd been kidnapped?"

"You mean you weren't?" Louise's tone was doubtful. "You mean you actually volunteered to go with him?"

Gabriella glanced up at Long John Christian and found him regarding her friends with tight-lipped apprehension. Annoyed with Louise for insulting him, she whirled to face the other woman. "Why shouldn't I have gone with him?"

"Why..." Louise stopped, her expression totally flabbergasted. "Have you already forgotten all the things you said last week about the bas—" she shot a hasty look at Christian and tried, a little belatedly, for tact "—about J. C. Lindsey?"

"Wait just a second." Had Gabriella missed something? "What does J. C. Lindsey have to do with this?"

Louise and Jack exchanged glances, but before they could answer her, Christian put both hands on Gabriella's waist and turned her back to him. He knew he'd better be the one to tell her. His voice was low and rather gruff. "I'm J. C. Lindsey."

For a minute she thought he had to be joking. "Don't be ridiculous. You're John Christian."

He nodded. "John Christian Lindsey. Most of my friends call me Christian."

Oh, Lord, no. Her heart sank to the pit of her stomach as she whispered, "You lied to me."

"Not exactly. I just didn't tell you my last name." He saw pained accusation in her eyes. "Gaby, we needed a chance to talk without all your anger over my editorials getting in the way.''

"I had a right to know who you are." She grasped his hands and removed them from her waist, then stepped back from him.

He sighed. "I was going to tell you."

"When?" Scrubbing her mouth with one hand as if to wipe away his kiss, she shot him a look of vigorous distaste. "You're even worse than I thought."

Both of them had forgotten the two onlookers. Christian brushed aside her protest impatiently. "You wanted that, Gaby. You enjoyed—"

"Don't call me Gaby! And don't you dare tell me what I wanted. You come here pretending to be someone you're not...pretending not to be who you really are..." She shook her head. "You do have a smooth line, I've got to hand it to you."

"It wasn't a line. Everything I told you was true." He gritted his teeth in frustration. "Gaby, listen to me."

"I listened to you all evening. That was my mistake." Part of it, anyway, she thought. The other part was that she'd looked at him, too, and touched him. Touched him and fallen...hard! The knowledge infuriated her. She drew herself up to her full five feet six inches. "I think you'd better go now."

Eyes narrowed, mouth grim, he stared at her as if trying to will her to change her mind, but she just tipped up her chin and tapped her foot in its dainty pink ballet slipper.

Her anger appeared to be every bit as enduring as his determination, and they might have remained in a standoff if Jack Grissom hadn't cleared his throat and stepped forward. "Look, Mr. Lindsey, Gabriella wants you to leave." His uneasy glance flickered down to the peg leg. "I'd rather not have to throw you out."

Just try it. The words were on the tip of Christian's tongue, but he bit them back, every muscle in his body clenched. Things were getting out of hand. He was about to lose his temper with this . . . this two-legged moose who felt compelled to protect Gabriella, and she was so furious at Christian for his deception that she wouldn't hear a word he said. He might as well leave and give them both time to cool down. Besides, he didn't want to finish this discussion in front of an audience.

Christian drew a deep breath and relaxed the fists that he had unconsciously formed at his sides. He gave Gabriella one last long look, then turned and walked out without a word.

After Jack and Louise finally left, Gabriella paced around her studio for hours. She was too keyed up to sleep—too nervous even to get any work done, although she changed into jeans and denim work shirt, plugged in her hot knife and made a halfhearted attempt at carving in some of the detail work on the chieftain's headdress. But out of sheer vexation she kept jabbing too deeply, and she finally had to put down her tools or risk ruining everything she'd already accomplished on the wax model.

How could that man have fooled her so completely? How could she have let him? He'd seemed so sincere . . . so motivated by humane concern for his fellow man. She'd bought it all and thought how honest he was. Brother!

She threw herself down on her bed and stared at the ceiling, wondering if he'd felt at all guilty coming here this evening. Probably not. More than likely he did this sort of thing all the time. Against her will, she relived the moments in his arms—felt once more the knee-weakening pleasure that had surged through her as he held her close. He'd been a firm rock-hard support for her . . . a musk-scented, warm-skinned man who had made her feel exquisitely beautiful and gloriously lucky. His lips had caressed hers....

Shaking her head, she shut her eyes, but his image didn't go away...especially the picture of him walking out the door. With tormenting clarity she saw his strained expression when Jack threatened to throw him out. She remembered the unspoken appeal in his warm hazel eyes just before he turned to go, a plea for her understanding. She had ignored it at the time. Now she recalled, too, the slight unevenness of his gait as he crossed the room. A feeling of shame crept through her as she thought of how she had stood by and allowed Jack to use his physical wholeness against her courageous pirate.

Her pirate? She must be losing her mind! She had better stop that crazy thinking. She needed to forget she'd ever been kissed by a dark and charming hijacker who'd plundered a large piece of her heart and carried it off as booty.

She reminded herself that John Christian Lindsey was the one who had marshalled the forces against her to prevent her getting the sculpture commission. Because of him, she was losing her last chance to save her grandfather's home. There wasn't even any point in completing the Comanche chieftain now, because barring a miracle, her career was finished.

Before she left, Louise had urged Gabriella not to give up. "The city council hasn't voted yet. You may still rally enough support to pull it off."

Gabriella just shook her head. Christian had done too good a job of pleading his case to her. The thought of old people and children sleeping out in the cold, going hungry, haunted her. If she hadn't been so blinded by desperate fear of what was going to happen to herself, she'd have realized a long time ago that J. C. Lindsey's editorials voiced the right, the *only*, stand on this issue. No matter how badly she needed the money, she knew that she couldn't solicit a commission when the community would benefit more from some kind of shelter for the homeless.

On Sunday morning Christian was up and dressed by nine, although he hadn't gotten much sleep and didn't usually go to church until the eleven o'clock service. He considered skipping church that day and driving to Bronte, planting himself on Gabriella's doorstep and demanding that she let him come in so they could talk. But then he glanced at his desk calendar and saw the notation about the meeting of the shelter planning committee to be held at Jay and Judy Templeton's house at noon. Knowing that if Gaby did let him inside, he wouldn't want to leave after just an hour, Christian figured he'd better postpone going to see her until the meeting was over.

After church, Judy served a big Sunday dinner for everyone, and then they moved into Jay's study for the discussion. Jay, who was a physician, and the minister Phil Schultz, had compiled a list of people they knew of who were in need of a temporary place to stay. Additionally, the major who headed the Salvation Army lodge in San Angelo sent word via Phil that they were filled to capacity and having to turn folks away every evening.

The committee's banker and financial adviser, Vince Perry, had talked to local businessmen who were willing to contribute to the shelter fund on the condition that San Angelo budgeted some money for the project. Kayla Newberry, one of the best reporters on Christian's staff at the newspaper, was writing grant proposals to be submitted to an assortment of foundations, in the hope of landing a substantial backer.

Judy Templeton had looked into a closed-down motel not far from the Salvation Army lodge and believed it was suitable for converting into a shelter if the owner would come down a bit on his rental fee. She suggested working out an arrangement with Major Haines so that the Salvation Army overflow could stay at the shelter and the shelter people could eat in the Salvation Army dining hall. That would save the cost of equipping a kitchen at the shelter.

As the pros and cons of each bit of progress were bandied about, Christian alone didn't express an opinion. His uncharacteristic silence generated quite a few curious glances, but he didn't seem to notice. When the last report had been given, Phil spoke up. "You've done a super job of keeping our dream before the public, Christian. I think we owe you the thanks for our growing support."

The others murmured their agreement, praise that Christian dismissed with a preoccupied smile. Eyeing him speculatively, Kayla said, "I understand you had a go last night at talking our would-be sculptress out of the running?"

That had been exactly what he set out to do, but the way she put it irritated him. "There's nothing 'would-be' about Gabriella Michaelson. She's an outstanding artist."

"She's also a beautiful lady," Jay said, "in case you didn't notice."

Judy was watching Christian with amusement. "I'd say our exceptionally bright newspaper editor noticed, all right."

He gave her a narrow look, a warning to butt out, but he doubted she would heed the warning. His friendship with the doctor's wife, and with Jay himself, went back too far, and Judy knew him too well. Ever since the days when she'd been the prettiest cheerleader in high school and he'd been the wild and sinfully handsome preacher's kid with a slightly wicked reputation, she'd been trying to sell him on everlasting love and marriage. She had worked to stir up a romance every time she saw him with a female and had looked on with varying degrees of approval as women like Kayla Newberry went after him on their own. Judy was holding her breath for him to lose his heart, and he didn't want her to guess just how much one night with Gaby Michaelson had shaken him.

"Did you have any luck getting her to see our side?" Phil asked.

"Ahh...no. I don't think so." He hoped his reticence would prompt a change of subject, but everyone just kept looking at him.

"You two seemed pretty wrapped up in each other as you were leaving the party," Vince said. "I tried to get your attention but you didn't even notice me."

"Don't tell me your notorious charm didn't work!" Kayla exclaimed.

Christian felt a tightening in his chest that had nothing to do with Kayla's barbed teasing. He shouldn't be sitting here talking about this. He needed to see Gabriella again, to try to reason with her. Checking his wristwatch, he stood abruptly and thanked Judy for dinner. "I have to, uh, take care of some business this afternoon. Let me know when we need to meet again."

He ignored the raised eyebrows as he bolted from the room.

Halfway to Bronte, he allowed the misgivings to creep into his conscious mind. Gabriella had been furious at him last night. And rightly so, he supposed. He should have known better than to keep his identity a secret, even for a few hours. He had known the moment she spoke to him that a single evening of her company wasn't going to satisfy him. He should have told her who he was then.

But if he had told her his name right off the bat, she would have suggested that he take a flying leap into hell, and that would have been the end of it. The rest of the night—

hamburgers, the shared laughter and conversation, the kiss—would never have been.

That possibility terrified him. In less than twenty-four hours, Gabriella had become a very important part of his thoughts.

With the same steely determination that had gotten him through some rough times, he psyched himself up to see her again. He would convince her that their differences on the sculpture issue didn't matter. He couldn't let her keep hating him.

But when he reached her farm, he saw that the garage was empty, and when he knocked on the door he could hear the sound echoing in the silence of the big brick house. He checked the studio, too, and found the door locked.

Thwarted, he sat for a while in the Jaguar in the surprisingly warm sunshine, tapping out a restless beat on the steering wheel with his fingers. When he'd been sitting there nearly an hour, he got out to stretch and wandered toward the house. Old-fashioned venetian blinds covered the windows, but he walked all the way around the building and found a couple of places where he could peer in around the edges of the slats. Idle curiosity motivated him at first, but what he saw inside made his stomach lurch, and he quickly sought another peep hole.

He made another trip around the house, snooping at every crack in the blinds, and then he leaned against the back porch rail, feeling sick. Every piece of furniture in the place was covered with sheets to protect against dust. Gabriella couldn't be living there! What had she done—packed up and moved in the middle of the night?

Straightening, he hurried back to the studio with its uncovered windows. The room where he'd kissed her looked basically the same as it had when she ordered him out. The unfinished wax model of the Comanche chieftain stood on the sculpting stand with her tools beside it. The bed looked rumpled, and a door he hadn't paid any attention to last night now stood ajar so he could see that it was a closet full of clothes. The pink ballerina dress draped one of the tall stools near the table.

Gabriella wouldn't have gone very far without her tools. She must actually live in her studio. Thank God. She hadn't moved. Christian began to breathe again.

"I can't believe it!" Louise tried valiantly not to laugh. "You really thought his name was Long John Christian?"

"I don't want to talk about it," Gabriella said for the tenth time since she'd started washing dishes from Sunday dinner at the Grissoms'. She heard her friend's muffled snicker and turned to glare. "What would you have thought if you'd met him the way I did?"

Louise continued to put away the clean dishes, her expression amused. "I'd have thought he was the sexiest hunk I'd ever laid eyes on. Which—" she gave Gabriella a knowing look "—is exactly what you thought when you met him." She laughed. "It's a real joke on both of us, isn't it? I mean, here I've spent all this time commiserating with you and neither of us had any *idea* what we were missing! Who'd ever have imagined J. C. Lindsey would turn out to be so irresistible? They ought to run his picture on the front page every day. I'll bet it would sell a lot of newspapers."

"Hmph!" Her unladylike snort didn't fool Louise. After thinking it over, Gabriella conceded. "He seemed so interesting—so romantic—I didn't really push him to tell me his name. I guess the mystery of the whole thing intrigued me."

"So you can't really blame him for not telling you."

"I certainly *can* blame him! He wasn't carried away by the whole encounter. He knew very well who *I* was."

"How do you know he wasn't carried away? Jack said when he walked in, you two were kissing. And I saw his face when you sent him packing. He didn't want to go."

Gabriella swallowed the knot of regret that clogged her throat. She had no cause to feel guilty. "I don't know about that. He didn't put up much of a fight about it."

"Who did you expect him to fight?" Louise demanded. "Jack must be three inches taller and thirty pounds heavier than him."

"Forty." Jack threw in from the living room doorway.

His wife whirled on him. "Oh...you! I wanted to throttle you when you threatened to throw him out."

The ruddy-cheeked, good-natured giant of a man chuckled. "You never should have worried about him. He looks like he can take care of himself. He has a few muscles of his own."

"You've got to admit, you do have an unfair advantage over him."

Jack rolled his eyes. "You and I both know I wouldn't have hit the guy. It's just lucky for Gabriella that *he* didn't know that...although I'm beginning to think she didn't really want him to leave." He sauntered across the room to the back door, shaking his head. "There's no pleasin' some women. If you'll excuse me, I've gotta go do some work on a tractor."

Louise turned back to Gabriella. "You know, I asked a lady at church this morning about Christian Lindsey."

Gabriella scrubbed at a pot with unnecessary force. "And?"

"You've heard the old saying that the preacher's kid is usually the worst kid in town? Mrs. Minter said whoever coined that phrase must have had the young John Christian Lindsey in mind."

Gabriella looked up. "His father was a minister?" She remembered what he'd said about sowing wild oats as a teenager.

Louise nodded. "Mrs. Minter said hardly anyone who knew him back then would have believed he would ever make it all the way to adulthood, much less become the fine, upstanding citizen that he is today. She said there was a time when everyone in town figured he was going to get himself killed in one of the gosh-awful messes he was always landing in." She giggled. "The more I hear, the better I think I like that sexy pirate. So what are going to do when he comes back to see you?" Her voice sounded anxious all of a sudden. "You aren't going to be unfriendly, are you?"

Gabriella bit her lip as she pulled the plug on the dishwater. "What makes you think he'll come back?"

"Instinct, my friend. And I told you, I saw his face. That man really didn't want to say good-night to you. Not like that, anyway."

"Of course not. He hadn't finished convincing me to give up the commission. I'm sure he didn't like having his sales pitch interrupted at gunpoint."

Disappointment clouded Louise's face. "You think that's all he wanted?"

"I'm sure of it. If he comes back, it'll be to try and finish what he started."

"But he's already succeeded, hasn't he? Half an hour ago you called that guy on the city council and told him you don't want the sculpture commission."

She nodded numbly, feeling doomed to fulfill her father's prediction that she would fail as a sculptress.

"So he should be happy when you tell him. And grateful." Louise sharpened her tone. "Gabriella Michaelson, you *are* going to tell him, aren't you?"

Gabriella ran one hand through her hair, smoothing back the untamed thickness with long, tapering fingers. Her wide brown eyes teemed with unhappy confusion. "I don't know what I'm going to do." One thing she did know—she didn't want any gratitude from John Christian Lindsey.

By four o'clock Christian had moved his Jag directly behind the house, out of sight from the road that led to the farm. Far beyond the point of impatience, he found it impossible to sit still for more than five minutes. As he strode back and forth between house and studio, he heard the sound of a car turning into the driveway.

In five seconds flat he was back at his own car, leaning one hip against the door in a casual pose that belied the thundering of his heart. When Gaby's turquoise-and-white Chevrolet sped past, he raised a hand and waved.

Gabriella saw the jazzy red sports car out of the corner of her eye and slammed on the brakes, spewing gravel beneath her tires. She swiveled her head and gaped at the man who lounged there like the king of the mountain, his glossy black hair ruffled by the wind. He was wearing a perfectly tailored gray suit and highly polished shoes—two of them—and the sexiest smile she'd ever seen.

Oh, Lord, she thought with a groan. It was too soon! She hadn't figured out what to do about him.

Four

At a much-reduced rate of speed, Gabriella drove on into the garage and got out of the car, then walked toward Christian reluctantly, aware that he was looking her over as he came to meet her.

Last night the frothy pink dress had made her feel special...or had it been that Christian's company had somehow inspired her with confidence? Usually she was reserved almost to the point of shyness and all too aware that she would never match her mother's rare Gallic beauty.

Today, in a loose-fitting scarlet sweater and a full, brilliantly flowered skirt that reached almost to her ankles, she felt a bit gaudy and very, very uncertain once more.

She looked just like a butterfly, Christian thought, his throat tight with admiration. The riot of colors suited her warm complexion and dark hair. Lord, her hair! It hung free and loose midway down her back, curling wildly, shining in the sunlight. A clip held the top and sides away from her face, but a few wispy tendrils feathered her temples and forehead. Her velvet-brown eyes studied him so steadily that he could only wonder what was going through her mind. Was she favorably impressed with his transformation from pirate to average man on the street?

They came to a stop, facing each other. "Hello, Gaby," Christian said softly.

Why couldn't she have managed to hang on to a little more of her anger from the night before? The smartest thing she could do was tell him to hit the road. It would hurt, but not as much as it was going to hurt if he touched her again and then left.

She struggled to rebuild her armor. "Did you want something, Mr. Lindsey?"

Mr. Lindsey, hmm? Well, he'd expected that. "Yes. I want to talk to you."

"Sorry but I'm busy. I have work to do."

Thinking she'd dismissed him, she headed for the studio. He was a step behind her as she went inside.

She whirled around and bumped into his chest, and he had to grab and steady her. His hands on her upper arms had a very unsettling effect on her respiratory system, leaving her all out of breath when he turned her loose. "I told you, I can't talk to you now. I'm busy."

"That's all right," he said easily. "I'll just watch you work." He picked up the ballerina dress and sat down on the stool, hooking his right heel on a support rung and laying the satin-and-net garment across his bent knee. He absently stroked the rich fabric as he waited for her to get started.

The slow movement of his hand and the contrast of the delicate pink material against his charcoal suit and swarthy skin mesmerized Gabriella. She could almost feel his subtly erotic caress on her flesh. She imagined his heat and her own pleasure.

Shivering, she tore her gaze away from his hand and moved over dazedly to her model. She usually changed into work clothes to sculpt, but taking off her clothes within a hundred yards of this man was out of the question. Even a closed door between them wouldn't make her safe from her own instincts. Nervously she wiped her hands down her skirt and bent to plug in the hot knife and heat lamp.

A second later she realized the futility of what she was about to do. She couldn't pretend Christian wasn't there! Trying to ignore him would be like shutting her eyes to a stalking panther. The danger was so real she could feel it buzzing along her nerves.

She dropped the cord of the sharp tool and straightened to face him. "This isn't going to work," she muttered, shoving her hands into her skirt pockets. "You'd better just tell me what you want to talk about."

"I came over to apologize for last night."

"You want to apologize for lying to me?"

"For not being completely honest with you," he tempered. His tone was humble enough, but he met her eyes directly, without shame. "I can't excuse it except to say that I already had enough strikes against me without announcing over the loudspeaker that I was your nemesis."

A beam of sunshine from her front window shone fully upon his face, bronzing it. Gabriella stared at him and asked absently, "What strikes?"

His sudden grin released a flurry of butterflies in her stomach. "Tell me, Miss Michaelson, are you in the habit of sneaking away from parties with men you've never seen before—disreputable-looking men who wear an earring?"

He had turned it into a private joke between them, a veiled reference not to his pierced ear but to his leg. Gabriella was aware that sharing such intimate humor with him only ensnared her more hopelessly in his charm, but she found she couldn't resist the teasing warmth in his hazel eyes. A smile tugged at her lips as she shook her head. "I'm usually pretty careful who I sneak around with."

"That's what I figured. I thought I should probably give you some time to get used to my, umm, earring before springing anything else on you."

She wondered if he really thought anything about his appearance the night before had bothered her.

"I knew you wouldn't go anywhere with me if you guessed my real identity." He leaned toward her slightly, crushing a handful of pink satin in his fingers, tantalizing her imagination. "And believe me, Gaby, I wanted in the worst way to get you out of there."

Her hands had grown moist again while her heart ricocheted off her ribs. Something peculiar was happening inside her, and she struggled to keep her head clear. Anger was the solution, she decided. Icy anger. "You wanted to persuade me to forget the sculpture commission."

He bent his head. "That was my intention...until I met you."

Hearing him admit it hurt. She turned away, her back stiff and straight. "The way I remember it, your intentions didn't change much after you met me. You were doing your dead level best to convert me to your side when Louise and Jack walked in."

He looked back up, his expression resigned. "I have a commitment to what I believe is best for San Angelo. I'll do whatever is necessary to get the shelter funding through the city council."

She clenched her hands into fists and spun around to face him. Her brown eyes glittered. "I'm glad we cleared *that* up."

"Gaby—" He stood up and tossed the dress onto the bed, reaching out one hand to her. "Gaby, just because I happen to be on the opposite side of the fence from you in this one matter, that doesn't mean we can't be—friends." When she ignored his hand, he moved toward her. "You're special, Gabriella Michaelson. I won't let you shut me out."

Tell him, a voice urged her. *Tell him you see his side...that you agree about the shelter. Tell him you're sorry it took you so long to face up to that. And while you're at it, tell him he's special too!*

He caught her shoulders in his warm hands and shook her gently, trying to make her meet his eyes. She lowered her head and focused on his black wingtips, giving Christian a close-up view of her smooth forehead. She looked young and vulnerable. He inhaled deeply, and her enticing perfume filled his lungs.

Slowly, with a silent groan, he tightened his fingers and drew her closer, at the same time bending his head until his lips touched her hairline. The silken texture tickled his nose, and he shut his eyes and smiled to himself, sliding his hands down her back to hold her against him.

His mouth skimmed down her forehead, down the straight line of her nose. He ached to taste her, to kiss away her resistance, but she wouldn't lift her face to his. Taking another long breath, he rested one cheek on the crown of her head, his arms looped behind her back. "Gaby, you feel this, too. There's no use fighting it."

She was afraid of that! Her entire body hurt from the tension of trying not to respond to Christian, trying to hide the effect he was having on her. Although her arms were rigid at her sides, she felt every inch of him where he touched her. She felt on fire with electric sensations that promised to deliver heaven and earth if she would only relax and accept them.

He brought one hand up and pressed his knuckles beneath her chin. "Look at me." When she finally did, he smiled. "I'm not going to just go away, you know."

"I wish you would. I have work to do," she said in desperation.

"Aww, Gaby..." His grin turned crooked. "You don't mean that." And before she knew what he was going to do, he kissed her full on the mouth. The kiss was so slow and sweet and laced with magic, it turned her knees to water and made her head spin. By the time it ended, she was clinging to him for dear life and praying he would never stop.

He lifted his head. "You see? I knew you wanted that, too."

Seeing his look of immense satisfaction, Gabriella felt her fury come rushing back. The conceited jerk! He'd done that deliberately! "Damn you!" Dizzily she pushed him away. "You'd do anything to get your shelter built, wouldn't you?"

His eyebrows rose in astonishment as she whipped out of his arms and fled across the room. He rubbed a shaking hand down his face. "What are you talking about?"

"You think you can get me out of the way by making love to me."

"What? Gaby, that's crazy."

She crossed her arms, breathing raggedly. "Not five minutes ago you said you'd do whatever it took to win."

"I don't have to kiss you to win the fight, Gaby. The shelter is gaining more support all the time, because people realize we need it."

"Fine. I'm glad to hear it. Now would you please get out of here? I have to get to work, and I can't concentrate with you leering at me."

For a second Christian almost choked, but then his sense of humor surfaced. The corners of his mouth began to twitch. "Leering? Is that what I've been doing?"

"Yes!" she shouted. "You've been ogling me as if you'd like to...to... Oh, Lord!" she moaned, flinging out her arms in a gesture of exasperation and then covering her hot face with both hands. After a moment she calmed down and dropped her arms.

He was watching her with a mixture of amusement and desire. "If I've been leering at you, it's because I would like to do exactly what you've been thinking. I'm trying to control myself, though."

His husky words called to mind all sorts of forbidden images. She had to wait until her breathing slowed down before she could speak, and then her voice sounded hoarse. "Control yourself somewhere else, if you don't mind. I have an art show to get ready for, and if you don't go away and leave me alone, I'll never complete all my pieces." The moment the words were out, she remembered that she would probably never make it to another art show.

"But we haven't finished talking."

"Yes, we have." She hugged herself as if something hurt her. "Please just go."

Christian's frustration mushroomed. For the second day straight Gaby was ordering him out, and he didn't want to go. She wouldn't listen to reason about the shelter, but that didn't bother him very much anymore. One way or another, the shelter would become a reality. What worried him was that he couldn't get past Gabriella's anger at him—a very personal anger. She wanted to be rid of him, and aside from making himself obnoxious, there wasn't a damned thing he could do about it.

He stalked to the door. "I'll be back."

"No!"

Scowling, he turned. "You won't be busy forever, will you?"

"I don't think you understand. There's absolutely no reason for you to come back here. I'd rather you didn't come back." She forced out that lie and then added an absolute truth. "I have enough problems without you complicating things for me."

Christian flinched as if she'd hit him. He gazed at her for a moment, not really seeing her, and then he shifted his eyes away and nodded once. Then, for the second time since he'd met her, he walked out in silence.

All the way back to town, he heard his own interpretation of Gabriella's words playing over and over: *I don't need your problems complicating my life.*

They hurt even now, ten years after that other girl had spoken them. Shelley had been in some of his journalism classes at Texas Tech University, and at the time he'd thought he loved her. Now he knew it hadn't been anything like love. But it still hurt, knowing she didn't want to get involved with a guy who had "problems"—meaning one whose left leg was removable.

Thanks to Shelley, his usually brash confidence didn't allay his uncertainty deep down inside as to how his friends really felt about his leg. He could convince himself that the people who mattered wouldn't be shallow enough to mind. But then someone like Gabriella Michaelson—someone who mattered emphatically—could come along and crack his self-assurance with one line.

There was, of course, a chance that Gaby hadn't been thinking of his leg at all. The night before it hadn't seemed to bother her. He hadn't noticed even a trace of distaste in her eyes when she'd studied him so intently; if he had, he darn sure wouldn't have tried to kiss her.

Christian tightened his hands on the steering wheel and
shoved the whole disturbing question to the back of his
mind. He asked himself what he'd accomplished by going
to see Gabriella, and the answer was, nothing. She wasn't
interested in debating the issue of sculpture versus shelter.
She hadn't been happy to see him and had unequivocally
told him that she didn't want him in her life.

Then he remembered that he'd learned one important fact
about her: she didn't live in the big house that had belonged to her grandparents, but in the relatively small, cluttered space of her studio. And he wanted to know why.

When he got home, he found a message on his answering
machine to call city councilman Bob Turnbow. Bob had
been active in screening the sculpture proposals and had fa-
vored Gabriella's work from the very beginning, but he'd
once confided to Christian that he couldn't put his whole-
hearted support behind an arts project at the expense of San
Angelo's needy.

Without enthusiasm, Christian sat down on the corner of
his desk and dialed the telephone. As he waited for Bob to
answer, he traced the contours of the small Michaelson
bronze that graced the desktop with his free hand, and he
thought idly that the palomino stallion appeared to be in
genuine flight, running for the sheer pleasure of showing off
his freedom. Gaby had an extraordinary gift for capturing
reality in motion.

"Thanks for returning my call, John Christian," Bob said
a moment later. "I guess congratulations are in order, although my feelings are mixed on this. It looks as if your side
has won."

"What?" Christian's head snapped up. "The council isn't
even scheduled to vote until this week's meeting."

"True, but there's not much to vote on. You've lost your
competition. Gabriella Michaelson called me this morning

and asked me to withdraw her proposal from consideration. That means the shelter's in."

Standing up abruptly, Christian clamped a hand to the back of his neck and kneaded the taut muscles. He frowned at the window, at the slope of clipped lawn he could see through it. "Why would she do that, Bob?"

"She said she changed her mind, that she's no longer interested in getting the commission." The older man sounded puzzled. "Didn't you hear me, J.C.? You win. You're supposed to celebrate, not question your good fortune."

"Yes, I heard. I just...she would have given us a helluva fine piece of sculpture, Bob."

"I know. That's my one regret about the way this is working out. I think she really needed the work, too."

Christian's stomach knotted. "What makes you say that?"

"Son, I'm familiar enough with the art market in West Texas to know the money crunch has hit there, too. Wealthy farmers and ranchers and oilmen are the only ones around here who can afford to collect expensive art originals, and when times are hard, they don't buy much. The artists have to market their work on a much broader scale if they hope to survive." His tone lifted. "But, look, she may not be in as bad shape as I've been thinking. After all, she backed out of this voluntarily. She wouldn't have done that if she'd been about to starve, would she?"

"No, I guess not." Christian ran the back of his hand across his suddenly damp forehead. Feeling exhausted, he circled the desk and sank into the leather chair. "Listen, Bob, this is, uh, great news. The rest of the committee will be delighted. Thanks for letting me know."

Hanging up the phone, he propped his chin on one fist and stared at the bronze. Great news, he thought, and wondered why he was gripped by such a sense of dismay. It was supposed to be, as Bob said, a victory for the economically stricken. Instead, he could only think of it in terms of defeat for Gaby. From some things she'd said last night, he gathered that she needed the commission badly, no matter how rich her father was. And he had a sinking feeling that she wouldn't have relinquished her chances for getting the job if he hadn't pushed her.

Why hadn't she told him that afternoon that she'd already withdrawn her proposal? When he kissed her, she'd reacted with that ridiculous accusation that he was making love to her just to win the fight—and all the time she'd known the fight was already over.

Maybe from her viewpoint, her suspicions didn't seem so ridiculous. Christian reached out to stroke the palomino's flowing mane and conceded that his actions had probably condemned him. He'd been fighting her with editorials for months and had lured her away from the Halloween party for the purpose of presenting his arguments to her in the best possible light, which meant withholding his identity as the enemy.

Gabriella had no way of knowing that the first time she spoke to him, he'd forfeited his soul. Nor could she realize that the worthy cause that had driven him for three months seemed like an almost unbearable burden to him now because it came between them.

But then, he reminded himself grimly, she'd made it plain he was a complication she didn't need.

Many more heart-wrenching exits like that from John Christian Lindsey and she would be a basket case, Gabriella thought. As she couldn't afford an emotional breakdown, she'd just better forget him.

Work had always been her salvation. Even now, when she didn't know what was to become of her, she was driven to her sculpting stand, where she labored until midnight Sunday, for the most part keeping her thoughts on the tasks at hand. With painstaking patience, she finished the last of the carving on the Comanche chieftain, etching in his hair and the smallest details of his facial features.

By the time she went to bed, Gabriella's head ached from considering her options. If she could hold out until the Tulsa show, she might make a sale there...at least bring in enough to pay the utilities and buy groceries awhile. Maybe even enough...no, she'd better not fantasize about solving the tax problem.

Anyway, she now had two new pieces that were ready to go to the foundry, and she needed yet another if she really planned to try to make it to Tulsa. As things stood, she couldn't afford the commercial-foundry prices, but a sculptor friend of hers named Nick Jantzen, who lived near Austin, sometimes let her help him process his commercial work in exchange for the use of his production equipment and his own foundry. But was there any point in casting any more new pieces when she still faced the likelihood of being driven off her grandfather's land? She didn't know; she was just too tired to think rationally.

Her back ached and her eyes burned from the long hours at the sculpting stand, yet Gabriella felt a gnawing emptiness at the possibility of never sculpting again. It was her life! A kind of desperate sadness filled her when she realized all she would be giving up when she quit.

The next thing she knew, she had let Christian sneak back into her mind, and she didn't know why until she thought about the pain that had burned in his beautiful green-flecked eyes before he left her studio that afternoon. They'd reflected the same heart-tugging sadness that she was feeling. He'd gazed at her soulfully, as if she'd just wounded him beyond redemption.

Why did he have to come back today and imprint his image more deeply than ever in her heart? Why had he looked at her like that? She wanted to put her hand to his cheek and ask him what made him look so sad, but she wouldn't get the chance. Once he found out she'd given up the commission, he would realize he had no need to come back to change her mind. He would quickly forget he'd ever met her.

She ought to be glad. Why wasn't she?

Five

By the next morning Gabriella had made up her mind; as long as she still had her studio, she was going to keep sculpting. She decided to continue her series of Plains Indians, which had received critical acclaim in the past.

After softening a lump of paraffin wax under the heat lamp, she began roughly shaping a human male figure about twelve inches high including its base. She was making steady progress on the torso when the ringing of the telephone interrupted her. Pulling a stool over to the kitchen cabinet, she refilled her coffee mug, then sat down and picked up the receiver. "Hello, Louise."

There was a slight pause, then a husky male voice said, "Not Louise, Gaby."

Her heart turned a flip. Why on earth was John Christian Lindsey calling her? "Sorry," she muttered, embarrassed. "Louise usually calls about this time."

"I see." He remained silent long enough that she guessed he was probably almost as uncomfortable about this phone call as she was. Finally he said, "Bob Turnbow told me you withdrew your proposal from consideration by the city council. Would you mind telling me why you did that?"

"Does it matter?"

"Yes."

"It's really none of your business."

"I know." His tone was subdued. "But I'd be grateful if you would tell me."

Her hand shook despite its death grip on the receiver. "What would you like me to say, Mr. Lindsey? That I'm a quitter? That I knew I couldn't possibly win against you?"

"I'd like to hear the truth, Gaby."

It was her turn to keep silent as she considered the wisdom of being honest with him. She sighed deeply and pressed her forehead against one fist. "It pains me to say this, but I realized you were right. San Angelo should take care of its homeless before anything else."

Christian thought it would have been easier to feel good about this if she'd turned out to be a quitter, as she put it. But he'd known all along that she wasn't. "You stepped down because of me," he said without any pleasure.

"Because you happened to be right."

"But, Gaby . . . you needed the job, didn't you?"

"I don't know of a sculptor who couldn't use a large commission like that one, Mr. Lindsey."

"Would you please stop calling me Mr. Lindsey?"

"Would you please stop calling me Gaby?"

"I'll try, but it won't be easy. I wish you would call me Christian."

She covered her mouth with one hand, as if he could see the smile she was fighting. "I'll try." Her answer sounded muffled.

"Good." He returned to the subject. "Is it true that you're having a hard time marketing your work?"

Her smile faded abruptly. "Please don't concern yourself with my financial situation, Mr.—Christian."

"I just thought . . . I'll be glad to help you any way I can with the business end of your career."

"No, thank you."

"Gaby . . ."

"Gabriella."

"Gabriella," he said impatiently, "why not—"

"Because I'm doing just fine." She softened her tone. "Really, Christian. You don't have to feel guilty about the commission. I'll survive. But thanks for offering."

As she hung up the telephone she thought that John Christian Lindsey should be required by law to bear a label in a prominent location somewhere on his body, warning that an encounter with him was potentially hazardous. Meeting him had to be the most unsettling event in her life.

The pervasive nature of Christian's influence didn't register until later that day when she had flexed the arms of her wax model into a fists-on-hips pose and was working on his legs. Suddenly she realized that this supposed Sioux warrior stood on what looked suspiciously like a peg leg. And was that a cutlass at his side?

Shaken, she stared at the wax figure as if it had come to life. She'd certainly never planned to immortalize the newspaper editor in bronze! It was scary to think how thoroughly he had maneuvered his way into her subconscious and made himself right at home there.

She closed her fingers around the malleable form as she considered forcing it back into a shape that wouldn't threaten her peace of mind. But then, of their own volition, her hands began to stroke the proud pirate as she imagined the finished piece on display at the Tulsa show, perfect right down to gold loop dangling from his left ear.

Her mouth formed a smile of anticipation. By gosh, she was going to do it!

Louise breezed in the next morning and slapped down a newspaper on the worktable. "Here," she said. "Read." And then she vanished as quickly as she had come.

The paper was open to the editorial page, which featured a color photograph of Gabriella at the Halloween party, looking every bit as beautiful as she had felt. She hadn't even been aware that anyone had taken her picture. The editorial heading read No Losers in This Contest.

With trepidation she read Christian's commentary and then went back and read it again.

Those who appreciate the rich cultural heritage of the Southwest have taken note lately of a sculptress named Gabriella Michaelson. A resident of Bronte, Michaelson was the choice of the San Angelo city council Fine Arts Committee to sculpt a life-size bronze commemorating life on the Concho River. The hitch, as most readers know, was that if the council voted to go ahead with the sculpture, it would have to veto the much-needed shelter for the homeless of our community.

Few people in West Texas enjoy the prosperity that abounded in the past. Those who used to earn a thousand dollars a week in the oil fields now live in cars and on the streets, and bronze sculptures are a luxury that many, even the wealthy, are doing without. This doesn't in any way reflect on the talent of the artists. It is simply a statement of our times.

That is why Michaelson's recent decision to decline the sculpture commission is so remarkable. Artists have bills to pay, too. Their inspiration may seem to come from above, but they buy their food at the supermarket, just as the rest of us do.

Gabriella Michaelson's growing reputation as a first-class artist is well deserved. Beyond that, her gesture of putting community before self offers proof that she is also a first-class lady.

Gabriella sat and stared at the words for a long time. Despite the subtle ache in her throat, she felt exhilarated when she finally went back to work on her pirate.

That week Christian did a little discreet detective work and discovered that Gaby would soon owe the county thousands of dollars in taxes. He also learned that she'd talked to a real estate agent about leasing her farm and that the Realtor had been unable to help her because farmers in the area were decreasing production, not expanding.

Still wondering how Gabriella's wealthy father fit into things, Christian telephoned his boss, the newspaper's publisher, Trey Lang, who lived in New York City. The son of the man who'd owned the *Journal* when Christian was a youth, and still a very good friend, Trey was happy to fill him in on scuttlebutt about the manufacturing wizard. "I don't think it's any secret that Andrew Michaelson has been trying to manipulate his daughter all her life. She just never quite pleased him. Some say she's too much like him—too stubborn, too independent—and not enough like her beautiful, submissive mother."

"Gabriella's beautiful," Christian put in quietly.

"You should see her mother." Trey sounded dryly amused. "Andrew thought maybe if Gabriella got hungry enough she'd return home where he thinks she belongs."

"You mean...he hasn't been helping her?"

"He hasn't given her one red cent in the past three years. And he says he won't, until she comes to her senses. Andrew's not really a bad sort—"

"Like hell!"

Fired up by Trey's revelations, Christian went to see Bob Turnbow to discuss the ins and outs of making a living as an artist. Unable to answer all his questions, Bob referred Christian to a personal friend of his, an agent named Maxine Presswell, who lived in San Antonio. Christian drove down there Thursday morning and took Ms. Presswell to lunch, then returned to San Angelo that afternoon with a notebook full of suggestions for boosting Gaby's career.

It wasn't going to be easy getting her to accept his help, he thought as he dressed for that evening's city council meeting. She had already told him to mind his own business. By now, however, he was beginning to feel she *was* his business. At least he would like for her to be.

At the meeting, Judy Templeton outlined the shelter committee's recommendations, and the council voted unanimously to establish the shelter, appointing Judy as unpaid director of the project.

The television station sent a team to cover the vote, and Christian was one of those interviewed for the ten o'clock news. The last thing the reporter asked was whether he thought the shelter issue would have passed if Gabriella Michaelson had hung in there and fought for the commission.

Christian tugged at his earlobe and aimed an engaging grin at the camera. "That's a good question. I'm glad it didn't come down to that," he said in his soft drawl.

Louise had invited Gabriella over for supper Thursday. They didn't eat until Jack finished a rush job for one of his neighbors, and Gabriella was still having coffee with the Grissoms when the news came on at ten.

During the report on the council meeting, all three of them sat in silence, eyes on the TV.

"Gosh, he's handsome!" Louise said when the story ended. "I saw Mrs. Minter again. You know...the lady from church? She said when John Christian Lindsey was fifteen it looked like he was headed for a life of crime."

"I don't believe it!" Gabriella muttered.

"No, really. She said he'd already been in plenty of trouble with the authorities when he stole a motorcycle and wrecked it. He led the police on a high-speed chase through the middle of town and smashed up against a telephone pole. That's what happened to his leg."

Remembering what Christian had said about motorcycles and telephone poles, Gabriella couldn't argue with Louise's facts. She could, however, express an opinion. "Mrs. Minter sounds like the worst kind of gossip."

"Probably half of what she tells you she makes up out of whole cloth," Jack said.

Louise was watching Gabriella. "Listen, I'm just repeating what she said, but I sure didn't expect you of all people to defend him. I thought you couldn't stand the guy."

Gabriella stood up to go. "I don't like to see busybodies destroy a person just for the fun of it."

"Oh, but Mrs. Minter claims to be a real admirer of John Christian. She's always going on and on about his courage in the face of tragic misfortune."

"What tragic misfortune?"

"Well...he's only got one leg, you know, Gabriella." Louise spoke with exaggerated gravity. "The poor man—to be so afflicted!"

"Oh, good grief!" Gabriella flounced to the door in disgust. "John Christian Lindsey isn't afflicted. I can't believe Mrs. Minter has ever spent five minutes with him. If she had, she would know better than to consider anything about him tragic."

When Louise burst into applause, grinning broadly, Gabriella knew she'd been tricked.

She narrowed her eyes. "All right, I admit it. He's not the jerk I first thought he was. Just don't you dare make a big deal out of it."

Louise wore an innocent expression as she saw her guest out. "I wouldn't dream of it. How you feel about him is your business entirely." Her tone indicated, however, that she knew exactly how Gabriella felt about John Christian Lindsey and approved wholeheartedly.

Gabriella had never made such rapid progress on a sculpture. Obsessed by the pirate, she worked on it almost nonstop for days, only pausing at night for a few hours' sleep and when Louise came over to visit. On those occasions she covered the true-to-life figure with a cloth and took out another piece to work on for the benefit of her audience. She could just imagine Louise's reaction if she realized Gabriella was doing a bronze of Christian.

On Monday Louise stopped by and invited Gabriella to ride into San Angelo with her to do her grocery shopping. When Gabriella begged off, Louise helped herself to a cup of coffee and stayed awhile. "Jack said if you want to bring your car over day after tomorrow, he can give it a tune-up. You'll be driving to the foundry pretty soon, won't you?"

"Maybe." As they talked, Gabriella carved intricate feather markings onto the outspread wings of a large bald eagle. "Anyway, my car definitely needs a tune-up. Tell Jack thanks and I accept his offer." She tried to curtail her impatience to get back to work on the pirate. He was so nearly finished—and so beautiful! Deliberately she forced her thoughts to other matters. "I don't know what I'd do without you two, Louise. I'll be glad to answer the telephone for you while I'm over there on Wednesday, if you have some errands to do then."

"Would you really? I'd appreciate it." Louise hated being stuck at home but feared Jack would lose a customer if she wasn't there to cover the phone for him.

"No problem. I feel badly that I can't pay Jack for his work. How's the business doing?"

"Things are picking up a little." The pert, freckled face brightened noticeably. "We've decided to start advertising in the *San Angelo Journal*."

"Haven't you tried that before?" Gabriella asked.

"On a small scale, but Christian says we should run several ads—a big one in the services section and others in the automobiles and farm equipment pages. And maybe stick one in the special weekend classifieds."

Gabriella stood with hot knife poised, staring in disbelief. "Christian says? Christian Lindsey?" At Louise's beaming nod, she put down the tool and moved away from the stand, brushing her hands on her jeans. "When did you talk to him about this?"

"Yesterday." Louise's blue eyes glowed. "Except for you, he's got to be the nicest person I've met since we moved here. He had so many good suggestions for Jack, for helping him get the business going."

Sinking down onto a stool, Gabriella frowned in perplexity. "Where did you see him to talk about this?"

"He came by the house."

"Don't tell me he drives around the countryside drumming up business for his advertising department!"

"No, he said he just wanted to introduce himself properly." Louise laughed. "Our first meeting wasn't under the best of circumstances, if you remember."

Boy, did Gabriella remember! "That's all he wanted?" she asked. "Just to meet you and Jack?"

"Uh-huh. As I said, he's got to be the best-looking guy in ten counties."

"I believe you said nicest, Louise, not best-looking."

"Did I? Well, he's both. I had plenty of time to make up my mind about that because he ate supper with us," she added casually.

"Is that right?" To her astonishment, Gabriella felt almost jealous, and her words sounded stiff. "I'm sure his suggestions are just dandy, but I didn't think your budget allowed for much advertising."

"It doesn't, but Christian said he's been wanting to check out the effectiveness of his paper's classified department. He worked out an agreement with Jack: free advertising in exchange for some input as to how much business we get as a direct result of the ads. Isn't that great?"

Great? It sounded too good to be true. Gabriella tried to be glad for her friends' good fortune and not dwell on the way she'd effectively told Christian to butt out of her own financial woes. After all, it wasn't his business advice she craved.

Christian stayed away from Gabriella as long as he could. Work kept him very busy, especially now that he was involved in negotiations for a possible buy-out of the Big Spring paper. He spent Sunday afternoon with the Grissoms and, thanks to Louise's loquacity, learned a lot about Gaby's struggle to support herself as an artist. He doubted if Gaby herself would have told him any of this.

The information would certainly help. After hearing about her experience with an artist's representative who had cheated her out of thousands of dollars, he would think twice before suggesting that she hire an agent. Yet Louise

said Gabriella would be the first to admit she had absolutely no business sense. Besides, sculpting was a full-time
job without having to worry about selling her work.

He sweated out five more days, worrying almost
constantly whether she could pay her bills, and finally, on
Friday afternoon, gave in to temptation and drove back to
Bronte. When he arrived, Gaby was so engrossed in her
work that she didn't hear either his car or his footsteps on
the driveway. Wearing baggy khakis and a huge pink-and-
black-striped shirt, she stood with her back to the open
door, her hand movements as she carved so fine that he
hesitated to knock and startle her.

After watching her quietly for a moment, he saw her lay
down her tool and straighten, spreading her arms and flexing her cramped shoulder and neck muscles. She half
turned, and he saw the satisfaction on her face.

"Gabriella," he called out softly through the screen door.

She had been thinking about Christian, having just put
the finishing touches on her pirate, and when she heard his
voice she turned eagerly toward the sound. The brilliance of
her smile quickened his heartbeat, rushing the blood
through him in a warm, energizing wave. He'd never been
so happy to see anyone, and if the look on her face was
anything to go by, she was glad to see him, too.

He opened the door and stepped inside. "Gaby, I need to
talk to you."

She needed to talk to him, too. Her smile faded as she
wondered whether they could ever manage to be friends. She
hoped so! Experience was teaching her the kind of man
Christian was, and she wanted to know him better.

Out of habit, Gabriella moved to unplug the hot knife and
switch off the heat lamp, and in doing so remembered that

her newly completed pirate stood in plain sight on the sculpting table.

Her brown eyes wide with panic, she grabbed the towel and tossed it over the wax model, but when she glanced nervously at Christian she realized she was too late.

Six

Christian blinked in astonishment, then slowly crossed the room and lifted the towel. There, in miniature, was an amazing likeness of him. He'd seen his reflection in the mirror often enough while shaving to know his own features, but even if he hadn't he would certainly have recognized the costume—the knotted bandanna with thick locks of hair peeking out beneath the edges, the single earring, the cutlass and scabbard, the peg leg.

He stared at it in silence for a long time, considering the detailed perfection of the wax pirate. Why had she done it? It was…he hesitated to label it beautiful, because it looked exactly the way he had looked the night they met, but deep inside he knew that description fit. It was clearly a piece she had put much of herself into.

He reached out his hand to finger the fragile cutlass, then touched the peg leg. When he lifted his eyes and met hers searchingly, he read the apprehension she was too distracted to hide.

Gabriella wished she could sink through the floor. Why, oh, why had she ever given in to mad impulse and sculpted Christian in a form that could be so easily recognized? Why hadn't she at least dressed him in regular clothes—something like the brown slacks and ecru cableknit sweater he had on now—and given him two feet? Without that distinctive difference, he might not have known it was himself. He was looking at her now as if he were trying to figure out what made her tick.

He slowly lowered his hand. "You don't get some kind of perverse pleasure out of sculpting a piece and then smashing it to smithereens with a sledge hammer, do you?"

Gabriella couldn't help smiling at his wary tone. "Not after I work on it for two weeks."

"You did this in two weeks? You're fast."

Shaking her head, she edged self-consciously away from him. She wished she had on anything but this psychedelic striped shirt that would have fit a linebacker for the Dallas Cowboys and sneakers left over from college gym class. Her hair was a mess, too—tangled and unrestrained since she'd brushed it early that morning. She hadn't spent much time on her grooming or anything other than work since she started her pirate. "It takes me a long time to do a piece, except when I'm inspired."

Christian's gaze intensified, causing her heart to tumble over a couple of times. "And were you inspired when you worked on this?"

Her vocal cords seemed unbelievably tight. "I guess I must have been."

"Inspired by anger?"

She swallowed hard. "No." Afraid of revealing too much of her confusing feelings, she added, "I've been hurrying to get ready for a show."

"You're going to put this in a show?"

"I hope to. If you don't mind."

He tipped his head to one side and watched her, rubbing his knuckles back and forth along his jawline. "I'm a little... surprised. I didn't think you'd want a permanent reminder of the way we met."

"I told you that first night I wanted to sculpt you."

"But an hour later you were ready to kill me."

"That doesn't mean I changed my mind about sculpting you."

"So you can dislike a person and still sculpt a flattering likeness of him?"

Gabriella moistened her lips, trembling inside at the risk she felt compelled to take. "I don't dislike you."

Christian didn't take his eyes off her as he closed the gap between them. "That's a start. Do you know of any reason why we shouldn't see each other?"

The nearer he came, the harder it was for her to concentrate. She tried valiantly, repeating, "See each other?"

Nodding, he caught her hands and pulled them so her arms went around him. Then he slid his own hands behind her and held her there, scant inches away. Her delicate fragrance filled up his senses, and he could almost feel her fluttering pulse. "Go out together. On dates, Gaby." He bent and nuzzled her throat. "Just like teenagers."

His lips felt like rough velvet and ignited flames of desire beneath her skin. The fire spread through every inch of her in the space of a heartbeat. She clutched him and said, "No!"

"No?" Without releasing her or lifting his head, he asked softly, "No, what?"

Her eyes were shut, her veins flowing with liquid pleasure. "No, I can't think of a reason why we shouldn't go out
on a date."

He straightened and, when she blinked open her dark
eyes, gave her a cautious smile. "Does that mean it's safe to
ask you to dinner tonight?"

Being in his arms made her crazy. Just his tantalizing
scent was enough to plant unforgettable fantasies in her
brain. His warm strength tempted her to act on those fantasies. "Safe for whom?" she asked breathlessly. "I don't
think *I'll* be safe."

His laugh was low and attractive. "Let me rephrase that.
Will you have dinner with me tonight, Gaby?"

Although she pretended to think it over, there was never
any question in her mind about what her answer would be.
She might as well accept it—she would have walked bare-
foot to hell and back with Christian Lindsey.

It was amazing what half an hour and a little make-up
could do for a person, Gabriella thought as she inspected
herself in the bathroom mirror. Christian had told her to
take her time getting ready, but she'd hurried to shower and
fix her hair, hoping he wasn't snooping around out there
uncovering her deepest, most embarrassing secrets.

But then he'd already seen straight to the bottom of her
soul when he glimpsed her wax pirate. He must know he was
getting some kind of scary hold over her.

When she came back out, Christian was absorbed again
in studying the pirate, but he turned at the sound of her
footsteps. The moment his hazel eyes settled on her, the
pensive look cleared out and they began to sparkle with appreciation.

Thirty minutes earlier she'd gone into the bathroom
looking young and adorable and sloppy. She emerged a so-

phisticate, in a khaki bush jacket with rolled up sleeves and
a belted waist over a lace-embroidered white linen blouse, a
brown-and-green Egyptian-figured skirt and classic brown
pumps. Her hair was done up in a loose knot, her face had
a fresh glow that was very appealing, and she smelled delicious.

Christian inhaled deeply and then decided that was a
mistake, considering the state of his libido. How was he
going to get through an entire night without ravishing her?
For two weeks he'd been suffering from wildly provocative
dreams about Gabriella Michaelson, and the prospect of
having her to himself for four hours was too good to believe.

It was a wonderful evening, Gabriella thought. The
weather outside was cool enough that they both savored the
intimate warmth of Christian's car. Riding along with him
alerted her senses to beauty she'd never before noticed in the
rugged countryside between Bronte and San Angelo. Never
again would she see the squat hills and lumpy cedar trees,
the twisted mesquites and oaks, without remembering them
as they looked with Christian Lindsey at her side.

"Do you miss Manhattan?" he asked when he saw her
gazing at the scenery reflectively.

She turned. "Do I miss living in the city? No. I discovered when I used to visit my grandfather that this part of the
country appeals to me. It must be in my blood."

"I imagine you came by it honestly from Eli Michaelson.
How long did he farm at Bronte?"

"All his life. He was born on that place, in the original
house."

"And your father?"

Her eyes took on a distant look, and she frowned as if
puzzled. "He grew up there, too, only he couldn't wait to get
away. He thinks New York is the hub of the universe. His

Southampton estate satisfies his need for country living, or
so he claims.''

Christian wanted to hear a lot more about Andrew Michaelson. Primarily he needed to understand how the man
could turn his back on Gabriella. "Has he come to Texas to
visit you lately?"

"No." She hadn't seen either of her parents in three years,
but it wasn't something she could talk about. Gently she
changed the subject. "How old were you when you moved
to San Angelo, Christian?"

Guessing he'd ventured too close, Christian followed her
lead. "The first time? I was fifteen."

"You say that as if you've moved here often."

"No, just twice. I came back after college and took a job
on the paper. By then my parents had moved away. Every
few years they moved because of my father's work."

"Oh, yes—your father's work." She shifted around to
make herself more comfortable. "Tell me what it was like
being a preacher's kid in small-town Texas."

He glanced at her. "How'd you know I was a preacher's
kid?"

"Is it supposed to be a secret?"

Christian gave a mildly derisive chuckle. "I should be so
lucky! Since my reputation always seems to precede me, I
guess by now you know what a devil I'd become by the time
my dad was assigned to the church here."

"Were you a devil?" she asked innocently.

"I was a bona fide hellion," he said matter-of-factly.
"And you can stop pretending this is news to you."

He went on to tell her about having lived in five different
towns in Central and West Texas before moving to San Angelo, and about his parents, who had been in their forties
when he was born. "Both of them believed in and worked
tirelessly for every worthy cause that came along. They had

their hands full with church and community involvement, so it's no wonder I was left to my own devices a good deal of the time." He sent her a rueful grin and shrugged one shoulder. "I could always think of something to get into. And everyone in town was usually watching when I got into it."

She felt a surge of sympathy for him. "That doesn't sound as if you were *bad*. Just high-spirited."

He kept smiling, not willing to correct her generous assumption about his past. He had been more than just spirited. For a time back then, Christian had been full of a terrible anger, at God and his parents and society in general, because he was tired of doing without—nice clothes, a car, all the things teenagers crave. Preachers didn't make much money, and his father was forever giving away what they had.

Christian hadn't understood then. If he had, he might not have rebelled and taken that motorcycle for a joyride, and things might be very different today.

Gabriella wondered at Christian's abrupt sigh and the sadness that flickered briefly in his eyes. Maybe, she thought, it was time to change the subject again.

Muffling her own sigh, she asked him about the progress of the shelter for the homeless.

"It should be operational in ten more days, thanks to a terrific director. Judy has managed to get everybody moving faster than I had dared to hope." His sudden smile reflected a fondness for this Judy.

Gabriella wondered if her complexion had just turned green. It was all she could do to speak civilly. "Oh, yes, I remember seeing her on the evening news. Judy Templeton, right?" When he nodded, she asked, "Have you known her long?"

"Mmm-hmm. She's been trying to run my life since high school." He gave her another slow smile, as if he didn't see the fire that was starting to blaze in her eyes. "Judy thinks she can boss me around, just because she's married to my best friend."

His ironic addendum made Gabriella feel slightly foolish about her jealous response. By the time they reached the San Angelo city limits, lights were blinking on in the dusk, and she had recovered her poise.

"I promised you a steak last time, didn't I?" Christian asked. "At Zentner's."

Not caring what they ate, or where, she gave him a calm nod. "That sounds good."

They continued to talk through dinner—filet mignon grilled to tender perfection and served with a bottle of Beaujolais and all the trimmings. Gabriella hadn't eaten on this scale in a long time, and she couldn't remember ever having enjoyed a man's company as much. They compared notes on books they'd read and discovered that neither had much use for television.

Already drunk on Gaby's presence, Christian decided against finishing off the wine. Every time he looked into her beautiful dark eyes, something powerful tugged at him. He kept inching closer...kept dreaming up a thousand excuses to touch her.

In guiding her to their table, he had felt a small-boned fragility through her jacket that reminded him of his father. That led him to wonder if and when she would ever trust him enough to let him help her. He was haunted by the thought of her doing without something she needed.

Hearing some friends call his name as they passed, he'd stopped to talk, keeping his hand on her waist as he introduced her. He felt both protective and proud of her. Then in the course of conversation during dinner, he managed to hold her hand long enough to examine the slender shapeliness of it, the long fingers with their short, unpolished nails. Although the palm was lightly callused from her work, her skin felt like satin.

Still not satisfied, he waited until she took a bite of the creamy rich cheesecake that they had for dessert and then leaned close and touched his forefinger to the corner of her lips, scooping off the drop of thick cherry syrup that glistened there, red and inviting. Smiling, he offered it to her on the tip of his finger, and she opened her mouth and accepted it without a word. Heat suffused Christian, and his thighs tensed at the moist suckling pressure on his finger. How he ever got out of the restaurant without embarrassing both of them would remain a mystery to him forever.

After they left Zentner's, he drove at a leisurely speed to the central district of the city and wound along the scenic Rio Concho Drive. He didn't know where he was going—he only knew he wasn't ready to take her home. Parking just across from the convention center, he sat for a moment looking down the grassy slope at the Concho River. Gaby moved in her seat, her shoulder brushing his, and murmured, "I've never been here at night. It's nice."

Christian agreed, his voice unusually hoarse. "Would you like to walk to the botanical gardens?"

Gabriella didn't want the beautiful night to end. She had a terrible fear that when Christian took her home and said good-night, she would never see him again. And yet seeing him, spending time with him, left her so vulnerable! There was a peculiar ache deep inside her, simply because the night would end eventually and she would be alone.

Getting out of the car, she joined him in front, and he took her hand as they began walking along the well-lighted jogging trail that paralleled the river. The warmth of his hand enveloped hers so possessively that after a few moments she stopped thinking about her fears and just felt. She felt alert and out of breath. She felt as if her nerves were just now recognizing a thousand vivid sensations that had lain dormant inside her for a long, long time.

They strolled through the first picket-fence-enclosed garden that they came to, skirting the white gazebo in the center, and then walked on down the river, paying little attention to the landscaping. They had the river walk to themselves, a fact that didn't escape either of them. It was all Christian could do to restrict their contact to hand holding. An emptiness in his middle reminded him of a need that had been growing in him since he first met Gaby.

When Gabriella noticed that Christian had started to limp, she wondered anxiously if she should suggest that they turn back. Acting on a brainstorm, she gave an exclamation of pain and held on to his hand for balance as she took off her shoe and rubbed the sole of her foot. "I must have gotten a rock in my shoe. I don't think I can go on."

Although Christian obligingly supported her as she acted out her little charade, he didn't believe her complaint for a minute. He had seen the sympathetic glance she'd slanted at him, and his first instinct was to get on his high horse and inform her that he didn't need special treatment...that his leg was more a handicap in the minds of others than it was in fact. Ever since his accident, he'd been offered more well-meant help than he needed, to the point that sometimes he rebelled and lashed out at the givers of kindness. But something warned him now that he could end up looking like a macho jerk without half trying.

He gripped her hand in silence until she had put her shoe back on, and then he continued to hold her still, his eyes unfathomable in the dimness. "Nice try, Miss Michaelson."

The low, dry tone of his voice had the same effect as if he'd accused her of lying. She gulped and stammered, "W-what?"

"That was good—that bit about the rock in your shoe." Before she could protest that she didn't know what he was talking about, he took both her hands and brought them up to flatten them against the rough warmth of his sweater. She could feel his heart beating steadily beneath her fingertips. "You're trying to get me back to the car before I keel over, aren't you?"

"I—I—" She couldn't seem to get anything out. Tears filled her eyes and glistened on her lashes in the moonlight. She hadn't meant for her concern to be so obvious.

"Sshh, sweetheart." He bent his head and kissed the palm of her right hand, then the left. A million tiny, very pleasant spurts of energy wiggled through her, drawing a shiver from her as he murmured, "It's okay. In fact, it's a pretty good idea for us to get back. My leg isn't going to give out, but if I keep going there'll be hell to pay later."

She sniffled hopefully. "You're not angry?"

"Angry at you? No." He gathered her against him for a fierce, tight hug that convinced her of the truth of his words.

When they got back to the Jaguar, Gabriella emerged reluctantly from her fascination with Christian. Noting the increasing number of cars passing by on Rio Concho, she commented on it, and Christian checked his wristwatch. "The roping events have probably just ended for the evening." He saw her puzzled expression and grinned at her quizzically. "Do you spend all your time working in wax, Michaelson? Don't you ever read the paper? This is the second week in November. The Roping Fiesta opened today."

She refrained from pointing out to him that the San Angelo Roping Fiesta was hardly a priority concern for someone in her position. Naturally it would be important to Christian, as editor of the newspaper. It was one of the top annual attention grabbers for the city, one of the largest steer-and-calf-roping events in the country. Every year thousands of visitors came to town for the competition, which was bound to boost the economy. And she knew how strongly he felt about things that were good for San Angelo.

He started the car and eased it out into the traffic. "Would you be interested in attending the Roping Fiesta with me tomorrow?" he asked casually, apparently too busy negotiating the curves to look at her. "I can pick you up at eleven for lunch, and we can catch all the afternoon events. Have dinner somewhere, then drinks at my place."

Drinks at his place? The very idea made her heart turn somersaults. "Most guys don't telegraph their moves twenty-four hours ahead of time," she observed with a lot more composure than she felt.

He did spare her a look then, his sensual mouth quirked with amusement. "I've asked a few people over to the house...not, I assure you, for an orgy. We usually get together to visit when they come to town for the roping."

"Are they special friends of yours?"

"They're nice folks. I think you'll like them."

By the time they reached her house, Gabriella still hadn't given Christian a definite answer, although the Lord knew she wanted to spend the next day with him. The next week, even. But she'd finished the pirate model today. Maybe she ought to get all her pieces ready and go on to Nick's, to get the foundry work done. The days were still warm enough that the bronze could be cast outside, which was the way Nick preferred to work. Maybe she ought to stay away from Christian for her own good.

After unlocking her studio door, he put his arms around her and pulled her close. She forgot the debate going on in her head as she breathed his scent, felt his hard warmth. She hugged him every bit as tightly as he was holding her and whispered, "I've had a wonderful evening."

"Mmm, me, too." His breath ruffled her silky hair. "What time will you be ready tomorrow?" When she hesitated, he said, "You know, Gaby, you deserve a day off. Even God rested one day out of seven."

The comparison made her laugh. She relaxed. "What does one wear to a calf-roping-lunch-dinner-drinks-with-friends outing?"

"You, lady, would look beautiful in anything. How about jeans for the roping? If you want to bring along a dress for later on, you can change at my house."

She pulled back to regard him with renewed suspicion. "How convenient!"

Grinning, he shrugged. "Or you can wear your jeans all day. These people will like you in whatever you have on. Just the way I do."

She started to poke him in the chest and ended up tracing her fingertip down the cableknit design of his sweater. The pulsing rhythm of his heartbeat made her whole hand tingle, and a responsive nerve danced in her stomach. Trying to ignore the distracting sensations, she grumbled softly, "You are a sly one, Long John Christian. Or am I just easy to charm?"

"I don't know about that, but you're remarkably easy to love." He sounded distracted. He didn't sound as if he were joking. And he kissed her quickly and left before she had a chance to say another word.

Seven

———

As Gabriella dug through her well-stocked closet the next morning, she mentally thanked her mother for sending her new clothes from time to time. Nicole Michaelson only bought quality, and because of Gabriella's life-style, her best clothes suffered very little wear and tear. She usually preferred comfort to style and dressed accordingly.

Since Christian had said to wear jeans, she donned her well-worn favorites, a chambray shirt and boots. Should she carry a dress or not? The question didn't require much debate. She knew she wanted him to see her in something other than just jeans today. Something pretty.

The closer it got to eleven o'clock, the more unsteady Gabriella's pulse became. When the telephone rang at 10:55, she glared at it, reluctant to answer, certain it was Christian calling to cancel. But slowly, gnawing at one thumbnail, she picked up the receiver. "Hello?"

It was Louise. In sixty seconds Gabriella had filled her in on where she'd been the night before and why she couldn't come over for lunch, and for the next four minutes she listened to Louise rave about the marvels of that man Lindsey. "I was just reading his editorial in this morning's paper about the inequities of our taxation system. Have you two discussed that, Gabriella?"

"No," she said, unhappily reminded of her own taxes.

"Thank goodness!" Louise chuckled. "I certainly hope you have better things to do with that gorgeous hunk than talk about vital public issues!"

The sound of Christian's car arriving saved Gabriella from answering. "He just drove up, Louise. I'll call you tomorrow, okay?"

"Sure. Oh, listen—tell him the advertising seems to be working wonders already. Jack's snowed under with jobs. Tell him we said thanks." She added with a wicked giggle, "Kiss him for me while you're at it."

But when Gabriella saw him, dark and heart-catchingly handsome in his jeans, open-necked denim shirt and boots, she could think of nothing but kissing him for herself.

"Good morning." He stepped inside when she opened the door. The husky quality in his voice hinted at sleepiness or suppressed pleasure or sensuality or all three.

"Hi." When she caught herself staring at his mouth, thinking about kissing him, she averted her gaze. "You're right on time."

"Mmm-hmm. And starving to death. I had to attend a breakfast meeting of the San Angelo Stock Show and Rodeo Association, and they kept me too busy to eat."

She pictured him taking voluminous notes. "Were you covering it for your newspaper?"

"No, I was on the program."

Now that had probably been worth seeing! "You were one of the speakers?"

Nodding, he moved toward her sculpting stand and stood for a minute gazing at the finished pieces on her shelves. How, he'd been asking himself, could he manage to get some of her work to his house?

He fingered a feather-decorated lance held by a young Apache warrior. "I like this, Gaby."

She got that special glow of pride he'd seen in her face before. "Thanks. He *is* pretty good, isn't he?"

"He's fantastic. Are you taking him to your next show?"

"Well . . . not him, exactly. That one is my artist's proof. I still have a couple left to sell of the five that I've cast so far." She opened a door in her storage cabinet and Christian saw a number of finished bronze sculptures, copies of pieces on the shelves; then she opened another panel to reveal countless plaster-and-rubber molds that were split, taped back together and labeled. "If I ever want to cast him again, I just have to find his mold and do it."

"So you could conceivably cast a thousand copies of a piece after just sculpting it once? That's quite an advantage over sculpting in marble or wood."

"Definitely, although I couldn't charge nearly as much for a bronze if a thousand copies existed. That's why I usually don't do more than fifteen in a limited edition."

His mind was hard at work, calculating how much Gabriella could be earning if she had someone to distribute her sculpture on a large scale—someone she could trust. After a moment he removed the warrior from the shelf and examined it closely, then turned. "Would you mind if we take this piece and some of the others as well—the mare and her colt, the Crow squaw and the Cherokee scout and maybe the windmill—so we can see how they look in my house?" When her dark, delicate eyebrows knitted together, he added with persuasive logic, "I'm interest in acquiring another of your pieces, and I'd like to see which fits best."

Gabriella stiffened, suspecting immediately that he had figured out how financially strapped she was. "No."

"No?" Surely he had misunderstood her! "This work isn't for sale?"

She thrust out her chin. "Not to you."

Was she joking? He studied her narrowly. "Is there something wrong with my money?"

Ignoring the question, she snatched the bronze out of his hands and put it back on the shelf. "I told you, there's no reason for you to feel guilty about that commission I lost."

He watched her rush around the room, picking up the calfskin makeup case and thumping it back down on the bed again with enough force to rattle the contents, then cross her arms on her chest and face him defiantly.

He crossed his arms, too. "I don't feel guilty. I wish you could have gotten the commission, but I would have fought you all the way if necessary."

"I know that." Her tone was chilly.

"Well, then, what's the problem?"

"I refuse to sell you a bronze just because you feel sorry for me."

Shaking his head, he rubbed a hand down his face in an eloquent gesture of exasperation. "That's about the craziest thing I've ever heard. In the first place—" he glared at her "—sorry doesn't have anything to do with what I feel for you. And in the second place, it's no wonder you haven't been making many sales if you put your potential buyers through the wringer like this. If I had any sense, I'd get out of here while the gettin's good."

Gabriella didn't move. What had he said—*sorry doesn't have anything to do with what I feel for you*? Exactly *what* did Christian feel for her?

Her stance still somewhat defensive, she said stubbornly, "The door's open. What's stopping you?"

Christian surprised himself by laughing, his good humor sneaking back. "I guess I don't have as much sense as I should."

He had no intention of letting her push him away out of whatever irrational fear was controlling her behavior right now. He knew damned well Gabriella Michaelson was as drawn to him as he was to her. She might try to deny it, but the potent attraction sizzled on both sides, every single moment they were together. It was even busily at work on his subconscious when they were apart, and on hers, too, he figured. After all, the pirate she'd sculpted said something about what went on in that mysterious mind of hers.

Christian uncrossed his arms and strode over to the bed, picked up the vanity case and the garment bag that lay next to it and turned. "Is this all your stuff?"

Looking uncertain, she toed a mark on the wood floor with one of her boots. "You still want me to go?" At his unequivocal nod, she added, "Then pick out whichever bronze you like best in the cabinet and take it."

"You mean it?" He gave her a devastating smile at his unexpected victory. "It will help if I can see several different pieces in my home, to see how they look there. I'd like your opinion on which one to buy, and we can bring the others back tonight. All right?"

Resisting the charm of his smile was like fighting the pull of gravity, but she looked him right in the eye and held her ground. "You're welcome to take several pieces to choose from, but only with the understanding that you're not going to buy anything. The sculpture will be a gift from me." When he opened his mouth to protest, she waved him to silence. "If you don't like those terms, the pieces will stay right here."

* * *

Gabriella stretched out on one of the matching blue-bronze-and-cream batik sofas in Christian's living room. With her head propped up on cushions at one end, she could see out the wall of windows opposite her to where the backyard sloped away down to the Red Arroyo Creek. It was a peaceful sight, with the long shadows of late afternoon shading the landscape, but she was too tired to take in the details. Her lashes drifted down, and she lay listening to the sounds from the kitchen—the clink of ice and the muted whirring of the blender.

When she felt the sofa cushions depress just beyond her long legs, she opened her eyes and smiled drowsily at Christian. Holding a margarita in one hand, he was in the process of picking up her booted feet with the other and propping them on his lap. He nodded at the low, square coffee table in front of the sofa. "There's your drink, Sleeping Beauty."

"Mmm, thanks."

Smiling, he leaned forward and put his glass near hers, then settled back and removed her boots. When he began massaging her aching arches, she moaned and burrowed deeper into the cushions, wiggling her toes gratefully. "That feels too wonderful to believe!"

He continued the caressing strokes without answering, and she became aware of the erotic nature of what he was doing. He had peeled off her thick socks, too, and was kneading every inch of her slender feet and ankles, lazily flexing them, subtly stimulating the sensitive nerves.

Funny, she thought, how the way he was touching her feet could cause such delicious sensations in other, purely feminine parts of her. Her eyes closing once more, she murmured, "My legs seem to be telling me they hiked twenty miles today. Is that possible?"

He chuckled. "Could be. We *did* look at an awful lot of livestock."

"Didn't we, though! There must have been six million calves, all of them looking just like the last one, if you ask me. Why people think they have to stand to watch the roping, I'll never know! If everyone had just sat down, we could all have seen just fine."

Clicking his tongue, he said solemnly, "One would think, Miss Michaelson, that you're not a genuine rodeo fanatic or you'd understand the phenomenon you just described. It's the same kind of excitement that comes over West Texans at a high school football game. The typical San Angeloan is physically unable to sit still between the hours of seven-thirty and ten o'clock on Friday nights in the fall of the year. It's a genetic trait, bred into these people for generations. It's what makes them such great sports spectators."

She laughed at his tongue-in-cheek explanation, but the sound choked off as he began to work with her toes individually, grasping each small digit between his fingers and pulling gently, sending spirals of pleasure coiling up through her. A hot, sweet yearning spread through her limbs as she lay watching him through half-closed eyes. His bent head and handsome profile with the glossy black hair boyishly disheveled made her throat ache with a feeling she'd never before experienced. She was falling in love with him faster than she could stop herself, and it was both the most terrifying thing that had ever happened to her and the most exhilarating. And she knew she'd better not give him a clue as to what was going on. John Christian Lindsey was without a doubt one of San Angelo's hottest—and most confirmed—bachelors. Besides, she'd discovered in the past three years that in the final analysis, she couldn't depend on anyone but herself.

The ringing of the doorbell shattered Christian's absorption with his task. He eased out from under her feet with a sigh of regret and went to answer the door, and watching him, she noticed that his limp was back.

Well, what did you expect, she asked herself, sitting up and running her fingers through her hair. If she was exhausted, why shouldn't he be as well? They'd been on their feet all afternoon, and she figured he'd been up since before dawn. At the coliseum she'd overheard numerous compliments on his keynote address at the six o'clock breakfast of the rodeo association. She ought to be offering *him* a massage instead of the other way around.

The open living area of Christian's home flowed around a centrally located limestone fireplace. By leaning to one side, Gabriella could see clear to the front door where he stood talking to his visitors, a couple of kids that he apparently knew from the neighborhood who were selling tickets to a school chili supper. She wasn't surprised when he bought two tickets and promised to see them there.

When he came back around the fireplace, Christian found Gaby standing and waiting for him. He planted his hands on his hips. "I thought I had just about put you to sleep. What did you get up for?"

"I figured this would be a good time to take a nice long bath." She gave a casual shrug. "You *did* offer a bathroom." When he nodded, she said, "Why don't you go do the same?"

His laugh was quick and dry. "Are trying to tell me something?"

"Just that you're as tired as I am. We still have to eat, and then you've got company coming later. I thought maybe a bath would refresh both of us."

Suddenly he knew what this was all about. He glanced down at his feet, then back up at her. "What's the matter—have I started limping again?'' Looking a little uneasy, she nodded. "Well, listen, Gaby, I hate to shatter your illusions, but I limp at least half the time. It doesn't mean anything.''

She picked up her drink and took a hasty gulp. "It's pretty obvious to me that you limp because you're tired, Christian. You need to rest.''

"I don't care how it looks, I'm not on my last leg." When her eyes widened, he added softly, "Come on, Gaby, that was a joke. You're supposed to laugh.''

"It wasn't funny.''

"Sure, it was." He paused. "Okay, maybe it wasn't, but I'm one of the few people around here who can get away with telling unfunny jokes like that." Her lips started to twitch, and he said, "That's better. I knew you'd come to appreciate my sense of humor eventually.''

Gabriella shook her head at him. "I think your sense of humor must be a little perverted.''

"Oh, it is, definitely." Lord, she was beautiful! When she looked at him like that—her eyes sparkling with suppressed amusement and all the sympathy washed out of them—he couldn't stop thinking of ways he'd like to pleasure her. Like making love to her feet, as he'd started to do earlier. And undressing her slowly and laying her down on his bed and then covering her up with his throbbing body.

"You want me to take a bath?" he asked abruptly, hoarsely. "Take one with me. Let's take a bath together in my hot tub." His hazel eyes were smoldering, thirty degrees warmer than usual.

Her heart stopped for five long seconds and then took off like a rocket. She dragged her gaze from his unsmiling face, to the V opening of his shirt where a patch of dark hair didn't quite hide the staccato hammering of his pulse, to the

TAKE 4
Special Editions **FREE**

Your introductory gift from Silhouette

Spellbinding and sensuous, every **Silhouette Special Edition** is a powerful and moving story of men and women drawn together by overwhelming desires.

To introduce you to this passionate series, we'll send you 4 Silhouette Special Editions, a set of 2 glass dishes and a surprise mystery gift – absolutely free.

We'll also reserve a subscription for you to **Silhouette Reader Service**, which means you'll enjoy:

- **SIX WONDERFUL NOVELS** – sent directly to you every month.
- **FREE POSTAGE & PACKING** – we pay all the extras.
- **FREE REGULAR NEWSLETTER** – packed with competitions, author news, horoscopes, and much more.
- **SPECIAL OFFERS** – selected exclusively for our readers.

There's no obligation or commitment – you can cancel your subscription at any time. **TO RECEIVE YOUR FREE INTRODUCTORY GIFTS** simply complete and return this card today. You don't even need a stamp.

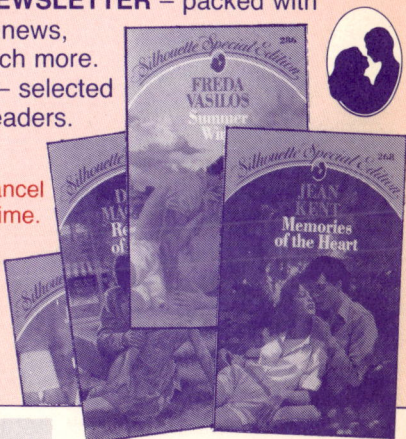

Return this card today and we'll send you these attractive glass oyster dishes PLUS a surprise mystery gift

Absolutely Free!

CLAIM YOUR FREE GIFTS OVERLEAF!

Reader Service
FREEPOST
PO Box 236
Croydon
Surrey
CR9 9EL

SEND NO MONEY NOW

FREE BOOKS CERTIFICATE

YES please send me my **4 FREE** **Silhouette Special Editions** and my **FREE** gifts and reserve a special Reader Service subscription for me. if I decide to subscribe, I shall receive 6 superb new titles each month for just £8.40, post and packing **free**. If I decide not to subscribe I shall write and tell you within 10 days. The **free** books and gifts will be mine to keep whatever I decide.

I understand that I am under no obligation whatsoever – I can cancel or suspend my subscription at any time simply by writing to you. I am over 18 years of age.

EXTRA BONUS

We all love surprises, so as well as the **FREE** books and glass dishes, here's an intriguing mystery gift especially for you. No clues send off today!

7S9SE

Name: _____

Address: _____

_____

_____ Postcode _____

Signature _____

The right is reserved to refuse an application and change the terms of this offer.
Offer expire December 31st 1989. You may be mailed with other offers as a result of this application.
Please Note Readers in Southern Africa write to: Independent Book Services Pty., Post Bag X3010, Randburg 2125, South Africa.

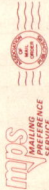

mps
MAILING
PREFERENCE
SERVICE

front of his jeans where she saw from the snug fit that a bath wasn't the only thing he had in mind.

She drew in a deep breath, stunned by the powerful hunger inside her that commanded her to say yes.

Witnessing her obvious inner turmoil snapped him back to his senses. Was he trying to push Gaby right out of his life? He said quietly, "On second thought, maybe that wasn't such a good idea. You take your own bath, I'll take mine."

She watched him turn and leave the room, and it took all her strength not to call out to him to stop.

Christian finished showering and getting dressed long before Gabriella tired of soaking in the tub full of soothing bubbles in the second bathroom. To remove himself from temptation, he went out to pick up pizza and had the table ready when she came in. She looked relaxed and unbearably huggable, wearing his white terry cloth bathrobe over very little else, her long hair still pinned up out of the way and the feathery tendrils damp and curling around her flushed face.

He stared at her until her smile took on a definite air of flirtation. The way he was looking made her feel alluring. "How do you like the fit?" she asked, spinning on one toe like a ballerina, giving him plenty of golden leg to admire beneath the hem of his robe.

"Want me to show you how I like it?" His own grin was devilish. He passed close by her on his way to the refrigerator and paused to emphasize his softly spoken warning. "Don't play with matches, Gaby. You might start a fire you can't put out."

In his crisp white shirt and black trousers, he was her special, personal pirate all dressed up, and he smelled so sexy, she almost stopped breathing. *Excellent advice,* she thought with a shiver. She wasn't even sure she would want to put out such a fire, which could prove awkward since his guests would probably begin arriving in a little over an hour.

They both made an effort to keep the embers banked as they polished off the pizza, talking about Jack Grissom's motor repair business and then about Gaby's car and its temperamental quirks and finally about Christian's Jaguar. Gabriella was astounded to learn the car was twenty years old and even more surprised to find out he had done most of the restoration on it himself when he was in high school. "I thought it was brand-new," she said, shaking her head in amazement. "You did a marvelous job."

"I did, didn't I?" he agreed with no false modesty.

"You were really only seventeen when you did all that?"

"And on crutches part of the time. If I hadn't had that car, who knows—I might still be."

"What? What might you still be?"

"Using crutches."

"Why?" she asked, frowning at the long string of melted cheese that pulled away as she bit into her slice of pizza.

He laughed and reached out to pick the trail of gooey cheese off her chin. "You're beginning to sound like a reporter. Who, what, where, when and why?"

"Well...why might you still be using crutches if you hadn't had the Jaguar?"

His shoulders moved restlessly, and he looked away from her. "Before Mr. Lang bought the Jag for me, I was full of undirected anger. A rebel without a cause. After my accident I'd refused to use my prosthesis because just about the only pleasure I got out of life was in making everyone around me uncomfortable." He met her gaze with a trace of humor in his eyes. "Don't you wish you'd known me back then?"

Wanting to touch him, to comfort him, she said instead, softly, "I still don't understand how having the car convinced you to use your new leg."

"It was simple, really. The Jaguar presented a challenge. It needed an awful lot of rebuilding, much of which I couldn't do on crutches, and Mr. Lang made sure no one would do the work for me. So—" he shrugged "—the car sat there, half finished and rusting, until I finally got off my butt and started walking again."

"Who's Mr. Lang, anyway?"

"He was the publisher of the *Journal*; the father of the current owner." Seeing her next question in her eyes, he went ahead and answered it. "He took a special interest in me because I had been one of his paper carriers at the time of my accident."

Actually, to call it a special interest was quite an understatement. Mr. Lang had eventually become a second father to Christian; he'd even gone so far as to provide a generous legacy in his will for his young protégé, which enabled Christian to live very comfortably on his editor's salary.

"Were you injured while you were delivering papers?" Gabriella asked.

His sudden laughter had an edge of irony. "Don't tell me you haven't heard all the details about my injury?"

"I've heard . . . gossip."

He arched one dark eyebrow. "That I stole a motorcycle and ran from the police at speeds up to a hundred miles an hour before I crashed?"

She nodded, feeling miserable to think that Christian was aware of the rumors circulating about him. "I want you to know I didn't believe that ridiculous story. I think it's disgraceful that people would spread lies like that."

"Gaby...." His voice trailed off, his smile more than a little rueful. "That wasn't a lie. I wish it were. I've wished a thousand times that I could go back and pound some sense into the teenage punk that I used to be. I wish I had listened to at least one of the good friends who tried to get through to me. If I'd listened, maybe I wouldn't have made some of my more spectacular mistakes."

Gabriella gulped, uncertain what to say. "What did they do to you? For stealing the motorcycle?"

"Nothing. I think they thought I'd already been punished enough. A policeman, who also happened to be a member of my father's church, came to see me at the hospital and told me he hoped I'd learned my lesson." Christian rubbed the tip of his index finger up and down his handsome nose as he reflected on that. "I'm pretty sure he spoke for not just the police force but the entire town. You could say I had a bad reputation." He grinned. "But I guess you already knew that."

When she just looked at him, Christian's grin faded. It might be inevitable that people would feel compassion for him, for his injury, but he didn't have to like it...especially when it came to Gabriella.

He rose and began to clean up their mess, speaking over his shoulder. "I'd be the first to admit you look beautiful in my bathrobe, Gaby, but unless you want to meet everyone dressed just the way you are, you'd better get moving."

After she left the room, he stood for a minute, worrying. There was so much at stake here tonight! Finally, rubbing the taut muscles of his neck, he went into the living room to arrange Gaby's sculpture to the best advantage. Once she discovered the real reason for this little get-together, he would be lucky if she didn't break his good leg.

Eight

Gabriella stood before the bathroom mirror for five minutes, summoning her poise. She supposed she looked all right in the outfit her mother had sent her for Christmas last year—a silky white peasant blouse and short lavendar-mauve-and-turquoise gathered skirt, with mauve kidskin slingbacks. She'd fastened her long hair back from her face with a couple of dainty combs, and her delicate turquoise necklace and earrings brought out that particular shade in her skirt.

The look Christian gave her when she joined him in the living room jarred her for a second, and she wished they were going to be alone. When he said, "Gaby, there's something we need to talk about," she experienced a fleeting hope that it might be sex.

But the doorbell rang just then, and with a distracted grunt he turned to answer it, his expression as frustrated as she felt. There wasn't time now for their talk.

An hour later she escaped into the kitchen for a few minutes' rest from the constant need to make a good impression. Mingling with twenty strangers—even twenty warm and friendly people, as Christian had promised her—strained Gabriella's social instincts to the limit. She felt so much safer in very small groups.

Still, these were nice folks. She was interested in getting to know them and discovering how each of them had become friends with Christian. Judy and Jay Templeton, Phil and Mavis Schultz, Vince and Marla Perry—all were long time friends of his from school or church involvement. Bob Turnbow knew him from his work on the city council.

Ranch owners, the Cavendishes and Greggs were in San Angelo for the Roping Fiesta; several other of the couples from out of town were in the oil and banking businesses. Most of them told Gabriella they'd known Christian when they lived in San Angelo in years past, although Eleanor Cavendish had confided that Christian's father, John Lindsey, had been their family's pastor in Lampasas when Christian was ten years old. "After the church conference moved John, we kept up with Christian through the years," she said, watching him across the room, her expression doting.

Gaby glanced at him, too. "What was he like at ten?"

Laughing, Eleanor turned back to Gaby. "Mischievous! He had more energy than he knew what to do with, and he was into everything. He's about the age of Frank, our middle son, and he used to stay with us at the ranch for weeks at a time. What a charmer! That boy could get milk and cookies out of me even when I knew he had talked Frank into sneaking out in the middle of the night to go fishing in the creek."

"Not your typical preacher's kid, huh?"

"Well . . . I think maybe he *was* typical. I've never known a preacher's kid yet who couldn't raise hell with the best of 'em. And I can understand it. Most children don't enjoy being made to go to church three times a week. And of course, with his father the way he is, I never found it very strange that Christian should go through a period of rebellion. Let's suffice to say that John Lindsey didn't give much thought to his family's corporeal needs."

Their conversation had been interrupted before Gabriella got a chance to ask what Mrs. Cavendish meant by that last comment. Now Gaby stood at the sink and stared out the window at the darkness, remembering how Christian had once mentioned that his mother had died six years ago and that he usually saw his father, who was retired and living in Kerrville, once a month.

The distinctive rhythm of his footsteps sounded on the brown tile floor, and his arms slid around her waist a moment before he spoke quietly in her ear. "Hello, beautiful. Are you hiding out?"

Closing her eyes, she nestled back against him. "Just for a minute."

He burrowed into her hair. "I hope you're having as good a time as you appear to be. You look right at home out there."

"I do?" Her doubt was evident in her tone. "I feel as if I'm on display. For the most part, your friends only want to talk about me."

"They're interested in you."

"Actually they seem more interested in my sculpture. I don't know why you had to put all the pieces out where everyone can see them." Before he could speak, she stepped out of his arms and spun to face him. "And why do you keep telling me to stop fussing whenever I try to get someone a drink?"

"Because I want you to just enjoy yourself. Judy doesn't mind helping me keep the refreshments flowing."

"So I noticed," she said pointedly.

He didn't seem to hear her disapproval but plunged into something that obviously had him worried. "Gaby, I think I'd better tell you that several of these folks are more than just casually interested in your work. They've been asking me about your prices."

"They have?" She frowned. "Oh, Christian, I'm sorry!"

"What for?"

"Because you ought to get to visit your friends without the hassle of answering questions about my work."

He looked uneasy. "I don't mind."

"Well, *I* mind. Listen, I think I have a few business cards in my handbag. If anyone is really interested, give them a card and tell them to call me."

He opened his mouth, closed it, then opened it again. "Gaby, several of them want to complete the purchase now. I mean tonight. It might not be good business to make them wait. Hope Warner and Jeff Gregg have already spoken for the Cherokee and Apache pieces, and Judy wants the mare and foal."

Surprise and overwhelming relief surged through her. "Are you serious?" She caught his hands and spread his arms wide, all but dragging him around the room in a dance of joy. With three sales she could pay the taxes and still have enough left over to pay the bills for several months!

Christian tried to slow down her little jig without putting a stop to her celebration. "That's not all. Leon and Eleanor can't decide between the Crow squaw and the windmill, but they definitely want one of them. And Bob Turnbow wants to see everything you've got at your studio. He's a serious collector, you know."

Speechless, she reached up to grasp the back of his head, her fingers plunging into the dark satin thickness of his hair and pulling him down to her level. The moment their lips met, a tender melting started in the pit of her stomach and spread lazily downward. After sixty seconds of his concentrated kissing, she doubted if her legs would ever recover their strength. Not that she cared, if he would only keep holding her...

Suddenly Gabriella was jolted by a familiar voice in the doorway. "I don't believe this! Every time Jack and I walk in on you two, you're locked in a clench."

They raised their heads, Christian looking sheepish and Gaby startled. "Louise!" she gasped. "What on earth are you doing here?"

"I was invited." The small blonde made room for Jack, who was pressing into the room behind her. "I think everyone else was invited, too, but you both seem to have forgotten there's a party going on." She shook her head at Christian. "I never thought I'd see the day when Gabriella would stand around and neck for hours on end, but that seems to be the effect you have on her. Would you care to share your secret with us?"

Although Christian let go of Gaby slowly, his eyes lingered on her. "I guess I'm just lucky." The potency of his gaze felt like a warm caress.

He moved to greet the newcomers with a smile. "I'm glad you could make it, Louise, Jack." The men shook hands, and Christian offered to show Jack to the bar. Just before they left the kitchen, he turned to give Gaby one more heart-stopping look.

When she and Gaby were alone, Louise began fanning herself. "Whew! I can still feel the steam you two have been generating."

"So can I." A rather dreamy smile curved her lips. "Louise, he's wonderful!"

"It's about time you discovered that. That man's the best thing that ever happened to you."

"I know." She turned to her friend, remembering her good news. "Guess what! Some of the people here tonight want to buy my work. Can you believe it? It looks as if I'm actually going to be making money again!"

"Oh, Gabriella, I'm so glad!" Louise hugged her. "But not surprised. Your talent's always been obvious; it was just a matter of connecting with folks who have the where-withal to purchase it."

Gaby floated around on Cloud Nine the rest of the evening, too happy to be wary of Judy Templeton. After all, she figured, anyone who wanted to own a Michaelson bronze couldn't be all bad. When they worked side by side in the kitchen, preparing one last tray of canapés, she discovered that the pretty brown-haired lady who tended to fuss over Christian Lindsey also loved and mothered her own husband and four children to distraction.

"It's a lifelong habit," Judy confessed with a grin. "Jay enjoys the attention, but Christian says I make him crazy, always trying to marry him off and bringing him chicken soup when he has a cold."

"You've tried to marry him off?"

"I did, but I won't anymore." Judy's smile was pleased. "I can see he's got a mind of his own on that particular subject."

"You just now figured that out? Haven't you known him since high school?"

"Hey, you have to understand, he never bothered to re-sist all my diligent efforts on his behalf. He always went along for the ride, not really caring one way or the other.

Until now." Judy picked up the platter and then paused. "I've never seen Christian look at anyone the way he looks at you." With those intriguing words and a wink, she bustled out to feed the guests.

An hour later everyone but Jack and Louise had gone, and they were getting into their coats. "Thanks for helping clean up the mess," Christian said, sliding an arm around Gaby's waist and pulling her over to his side where he leaned against the fireplace wall.

"Don't mention it." Louise and Jack spoke together.

"That's what they always say," Gabriella told Christian softly, then looked at her friends. "After I deposit those checks in my bank, the first debt I'm going to pay off is the one I owe you for all the work Jack's done on my car."

Jack reddened to the roots of his fair hair. "Forget it."

"You know he never expected to get paid for that," Louise said. "What are friends for? I'm just glad Christian's brainstorm worked out as well for you as his advertising schemes are working for us. He was a little worried that you might get mad."

Feeling Christian stiffen beside her, Gaby pulled back to study his guilt-ridden expression. She didn't have the slightest idea what Louise could be talking about.

Her friend chattered on, paying more attention to buttoning her coat than she was to Christian's tension and Gabriella's dawning frown. "I told him you'd have to be a nitwit to get upset at him for wanting to help you. Especially since I've heard you say it's common practice for art patrons to host parties for sculptors and invite potential buyers. And it really paid off tonight, didn't it?"

When total silence followed her question, Louise glanced up and saw the disbelief on Gaby's face. Then, covering her mouth with her hand, Louise turned stricken eyes on

Christian, who was looking a little pale. "Gosh, I'm sorry! I thought she knew, Christian. I'm so sorry!"

He shook his head mutely, finding no words to tell her it was all right. It wasn't all right. Gaby was going to kill him. But that wasn't Louise's fault. It was his own damn-blasted fault for not talking this over with Gaby before he set it up. Or at least for not telling her before everyone arrived that this was really her party, not his.

But if he *had* talked it over with Gaby, she would have said no in terms that he couldn't argue with. And she wouldn't have made those four sales, and she wouldn't be thousands of dollars richer right now than she had been yesterday.

And she also wouldn't be looking at him as if he were some kind of revolting creature she might find under a rock.

Vaguely he heard Jack whisper something to Louise, and then Louise said miserably, "We'd better go and let you two work this out."

Gabriella didn't answer. She turned away and left the room, going straight to the guest bedroom to gather up her garment bag and makeup case. When she came back to the living room, Christian was closing the front door and they were alone.

Coming face-to-face with him, she halted and gave him an icy stare. When he reached out as if to relieve her of the things she was carrying, she gripped them tighter and jerked back out of his reach. "You should have told Jack and Louise to wait for me. It would have saved you a long drive," she said coolly.

He made no move to get his coat or car keys. "I'm not taking you home until we talk about this."

"Okay, I'll walk." And she started for the door, disregarding the fact that it would probably take her a week to walk home from San Angelo.

"No, you damn well won't," he snapped, stepping into her path and taking the two bags out of her hands before she could stop him. He dumped them on a chair nearby and then grasped her arm and propelled her over to the couch, forcibly seating her there despite her resistance. She glared at him, breathing raggedly, and he crossed his arms and looked right back at her. "Go ahead and say it, Gaby. Get it all out. Tell me what you're feeling."

The fury and hurt exploded out of her. "You . . . you . . . jerk! You sneaky underhanded manipulative creep! How dare you trick me like that? How could you let me make such a fool of myself?" She had thought those people were starting to like her; she'd certainly never dreamed that they'd bought the pieces as a favor to Christian.

As he watched, tears filled her dark eyes, and each glistening drop twisted the knife of regret deeper in his stomach. He sat down beside her. "Gaby—"

"I'm not through," she gritted hoarsely. He reached to wipe her cheeks, but she scooted down the sofa as far as she could get from him. "You want to know what I feel? I feel tricked. I feel incredibly stupid." She scrubbed at the tears herself then with shaking fingers. "I can't believe I was so blind! I was the only one here tonight who didn't know what was going on. It must have been pretty funny. I hope it gave everyone something to laugh about on their way home."

"Gaby, that's ridiculous," he interrupted, standing up and pacing around the room. "Nobody laughed at you. Everyone thought you were wonderful. I knew they would. That's why I wanted you to meet them. And they loved your art."

"Oh come on, Lindsey! You wanted me to meet them so you could get me off your conscience. Well, you pulled it off, didn't you? You did your good deed for the day and saved the poor struggling artist from a fate worse than death.''

He stepped in front of the hearth and stood with his legs braced apart, his mouth tight. "I told you this morning that I don't feel sorry for you, Gaby."

"You expect me to believe you haven't pitied me for being on the verge of losing my grandfather's farm?"

Reluctantly he said, "I worry about you."

"Well, don't. As *I* told *you* this morning, I don't need your help."

Lord, she was stubborn! "Why is it all right for Jack to fix your car but it's not okay for me to invite some people to look at your work? People that I wanted you to meet anyway."

"It's okay for Jack to fix my car because he and Louise are my friends. They know I'll help them whenever I can."

A steel band seemed to be constricting his breathing. "And I'm not a friend?"

"Friends are honest with each other," she muttered. "Friends don't scheme behind each other's backs."

He stalked to a chair and sat. Pressing his shoulders back and flexing his neck, he exhaled as he looked at her. "I admit I should have talked to you about the party when the idea first occurred to me, but I knew what your reaction would be. You would have refused to let me invite anyone, and damn it all, Gaby, you needed those sales!"

"That should have been my decision, not yours. If I can't make it on my own, I don't want to make it at all."

"That's absurd!" He sounded grimly amused. "You've acknowledged that these parties are standard practice. You've finally even admitted you can use the money. But you would still have turned down flat my offer to help out of mule-headed pride. If you can't see the stupidity of that, you must *really* be blind." Hazel eyes turbulent, he reached up and thrust the fingers of his left hand through his dark hair. "It makes about as much sense as my insistence on using crutches when I could have been walking. The solution to my problem was right there all along, but I thought I had to do things the hard way."

"Thank you for that brilliant commentary on my behaviour, Dr. Freud." His words stung, and not for the world would she have admitted that he could be right. "I don't know how I got by for twenty-three years before you took it upon yourself to direct my life."

Christian lowered his hand to his knee and rubbed it absently. After a moment he got to his feet and picked up her things from the next chair. "I'll take you home now if you're ready," he said, his voice even.

There was plenty more he could say to her. Plenty he would like to tell her about the not always rational fears that can drive a person to cut off his nose to spite his face. But maybe that was something Gaby was going to have to come to terms with herself.

Anyway, he had to be careful not to anger her any more than he'd already done. So far she hadn't threatened to return—or worse yet, to tear up—the checks for her pieces of bronze. Maybe it hadn't occurred to her to do so, and he didn't want to give her any ideas. She'd earned that money, and she needed it in a bad way. Christian intended to see that she kept it, even if . . . Lord help him, even if that meant he never got to come near her again.

As the Jaguar streaked along the black highway toward Bronte, Gabriella huddled in the soft red leather seat as far as she could get from Christian and his bewitching fragrance. Not that she could escape it; the whole car was indelibly stamped with his scent and personality.

Her stomach churned with the smoldering remains of her anger, but that didn't entirely explain why she felt so miserable. One thing she knew—until her path crossed John Christian Lindsey's, she hadn't been subjected to the breathless highs and lows that had traumatized her these past few weeks. She would be much better off never seeing him again. In fact, she was going to do everything possible to settle back into the familiar, if sometimes boring, routine that had characterized her life a month ago. If she was lucky, she could forget she'd ever met Christian.

Nine

The next morning Gabriella packed a few clothes and carefully loaded her latest wax models into her car. During the long, sleepless night she had convinced herself she must leave for the foundry at once in order to cast her new pieces in time for the Tulsa show. The fact that her leaving would remove her from a painful relationship was irrelevant, or at least so she told herself.

Although she considered calling Louise before she left, she didn't want to face her inevitable questions. Besides, she was annoyed that Louise hadn't warned her about the purpose of Christian's party. In fact, Louise hadn't even admitted that she and Jack were going to the party when she'd called Gaby Saturday morning. It would serve her right if she had to wonder where Gaby was for a while.

Then Gaby remembered all the meals the Grissoms had shared with her and the dress Louise had made for the Halloween party and the countless other ways in which their friendship had blossomed, and she knew she couldn't punish Louise and Jack for something that had been Christian's doing. She would write them a note and drop it in their mailbox on her way out of town.

Christian intended to give Gaby time to cool down, but by Monday noon he missed her so much that he gave in and tried to call her. There was no answer. He kept trying all afternoon, and by the time he left his office at five-thirty, he was starting to worry. He went home and changed clothes, dialing her number one last time. When she still didn't answer, he got in his car and drove to her farm.

Her car was gone and the studio door locked. Peering through the windows, he saw that the wax pirate model was missing from the sculpting stand. That, he decided, was not a good sign. Considering her mood on Saturday night, she might very well have stuck the pirate in the oven and turned on the heat. He sincerely hoped that hadn't been the fate of his look-alike, because if it had, Christian's own chances of surviving this latest development unscathed probably weren't very good.

After still not being able to reach Gaby all day Tuesday, he finally conceded defeat and called Louise. "I've been worried about how things went after we left the other night," she said. "Did Gabriella come to her senses?"

"She didn't throw her arms around me and thank me for my trouble, if that's what you mean," he said dryly. "Haven't you asked her about it?"

"I haven't seen her since the party, or you can be darn sure I would have asked. She's taken her wax models to a foundry to be cast. It's down close to Austin, near Marble Falls."

Louise told him about finding the note from Gaby along with the checks and a request for Louise to deposit them in Gaby's bank account on Monday.

Profoundly relieved to learn that Gaby was going to keep the money, Christian asked, "Is this foundry the nearest one to Bronte?"

"No. She goes there because it belongs to a sculptor friend of hers, a guy named Nick Jantzen. He lets her use his equipment in exchange for her help on his commercial work."

His good mood faded. "How long have they had this arrangement?"

"Several years. If Nick hadn't helped her, she probably couldn't have afforded to cast any pieces since the market got so tight."

Christian supposed he should be glad Gaby had such a generous friend, but he would have been a lot happier if he had some reassurance that friendship was as far as things went between them.

"Where's she staying? I'll call her at her motel later tonight."

"She's staying with Nick." Christian's sudden taut silence spoke volumes, and Louise added with a chuckle, "In his guest room. Nick's like an uncle to her."

"How old is this guy?" he asked suspiciously.

"Ancient. At least fifty."

"Fifty isn't ancient."

"Well, whatever he is, he's much too old for Gabriella. He's gray-haired and portly. I doubt if he has all his teeth."

He grunted. "If he has all his limbs, he's got me beat."

"Christian!" Louise blurted in shock. "John Christian Lindsey, you know better than that! I can't believe you said anything so stupid."

After a moment of uncomfortable silence, he released a deep sigh. "Sorry. I shouldn't have let that slip out."

"You shouldn't even think it. It doesn't matter to anyone."

"Listen, Louise—" he returned doggedly to the subject "—have you ever laid eyes on this Nick character? Or are you just fabricating his advanced age to try to convince me that I might still have a chance with Gaby?"

"I haven't actually seen him, and Gabriella's never mentioned his age. I'm positive she doesn't think of him the way you're thinking she does." She paused to let him sort that out and then spoke with her usual candor. "Before I assure you that Gabriella finds you very sexy, I think I ought to ask just exactly what *your* intentions are concerning my best friend. Because I've gotta tell you, she doesn't need any more problems."

"The last thing I want to do is cause problems for Gaby."

"Then what do you want?"

The question defied Christian. He was still searching for the answer himself. Sighing again, he said, "I don't know for sure. I just know I want to be part of her life."

"On exactly what terms?"

Louise sounded so much like a lawyer grilling a witness, Christian smiled wryly to himself. "Oh whatever terms she'll have me. Right now it looks as if I'm out."

"Then I guess it's up to you to get back in, isn't it?"

"Believe me, I intend to. How long will she be at the foundry?"

"A couple of weeks."

He grimaced. "Don't tell me she's staying through Thanksgiving!"

"I don't know for sure. Why don't you call her and ask?"

He wrote down the number and thanked Louise.

"You know, Christian, you could always drop in on them for Thanksgiving dinner," she suggested, only half teasing.

"Sure. Me and Gabriella and Uncle Nick. That should be cozy."

"Why not?" she asked with a laugh. "You're the one she thinks is sexy."

"Hmph. I'm also the one who pulled a fast number on her the other night. It'll take some doing to earn her forgiveness this time."

"Just remember, she's keeping the money. That must mean something."

Christian hoped Louise was right.

Gabriella and Nick had worked together often enough in the past to be able to settle into a smooth routine. As the two of them plus Nick's crew of helpers went through the many steps necessary to create the molds which would eventually take the bronze, they worked mostly in silence and made speedy progress.

One good thing about this phase of the production process was that Gaby's mind could wander far afield without slowing her down. And wander it did. She brooded over Christian Lindsey for hours at a time, particularly when she was preparing the mother mold and then the ceramic shell for her pirate. She missed the man, more than she would ever have believed she could miss anyone. She missed everything about him. It was funny how suddenly she couldn't stop recalling all the things about him that she liked. His lean, dark and handsome looks were definitely a factor, but only one of many. There was so much more about him that captivated her mind and her heart: his warm, appealing personality and sense of humor, his dedication to excellence in his work, his refusal to feel sorry for himself, his generosity and sincere concern for others.

The thought that she wouldn't be seeing him again created a huge emptiness inside her that she suspected would only stop hurting if she let Christian come back into her life and fill it up. And that was a possibility she couldn't even consider. She'd been pushing herself for three years to prove that she didn't need a man behind her to succeed as a sculptor. No matter how wonderful he was otherwise, she didn't need a man at all if he didn't treat her as his equal.

Why, Gabriella asked herself, couldn't Christian treat her more like Nick did? Nick expected her to carry her own weight at the foundry, and he would never have pulled a condescending stunt like setting up a party for potential buyers without Gaby's permission.

Unlike the man Louise had described to Christian, the real Nick Jantzen was just six years older than Gabriella and in excellent physical condition. He had to be to do all the heavy lifting involved in pouring bronze. His skin stayed tan all year long, and his brown hair was sun-streaked from working outside at the smelter, heating the bronze. He had the kind of good looks that made a subtle but lasting impression on women, as evidenced by the sultry looks he got from the numerous females on his foundry work staff.

It amused Gabriella to see the way Nick tended to ignore the flirtations. He didn't seem to notice whether his workers were male or female, and he always managed to keep his mind on the job he was doing. And he was very good at his work.

Gaby had met him at an art show in Austin. The same people showed up at all the shows, often sharing campers and pots of stew, forming a network of friendships that gave them the moral support they needed to survive the frequently isolated existence of hard-working artists. In their quiet talks at subsequent shows, Gabriella and Nick had developed a friendship based on common interest and mutual respect.

Despite the fact that she never complained, Nick had suspected what a tough time Gabriella was having. Soon after that he had invited her to cast some of her pieces at his own private foundry in a beautiful wooded location right on Lake Marble Falls. Rumor had it he'd received a large inheritance that would support him comfortably the rest of his life, but Gaby didn't know if that was true because Nick never talked about money.

At least he never talked about his own money. And he'd never talked about hers, either, until this trip. Then, one night after they'd finished working on the ceramic shells and were sitting in front of a fire, without saying much himself he somehow got Gabriella to open up. Before she knew it, she'd told him not just about her constant worry over expenses, but also about her misguided battle for the sculpture commission. *And* she'd told him about John Christian Lindsey and all his devious tricks.

Nick was a good listener. He watched her face as she talked, which made her self-conscious when she first began. But then as she warmed up, she lost track of everything. A tumultuous storm of emotions swept through her as she described all that had happened from Christian's first editorial on the subject of sculpture until the embarrassing discovery she'd made at his party.

When she finished, she felt totally drained but satisfied with her word portrait of a charming manipulator who'd conned his way into her life and turned it upside down. Leaning back against the sofa, she looked at Nick expectantly. "Well? What do you think?"

Gaby's first clue that Nick wasn't in complete agreement with her came when he didn't answer right away. He was sitting near the fireplace, and he took the time to throw another log on the fire before he propped both elbows on his knees and steepled his hands together, leaning forward to regard her over the tips of his fingers. "I've been wondering when this was going to happen."

"When what was going to happen?"

"When you were going to fall in love. In all the time we've known each other, I've never seen you take a second look at a man. You didn't even fall for me." He grinned. "And not because I didn't try."

She sat up straight in exasperation. "Nick, would you stop kidding around? Didn't you hear a word I said? I want your honest opinion. Am I right or wrong?"

"Come on, Gabriella. You don't want honesty—you want sympathy. And no wonder. You've got it bad for this . . . this Christian."

Standing, she stomped into the kitchen to get a mug of hot cider and poured one for Nick while she was at it. When she handed him his cup and sat back down, she said, "I'll admit I let him get a little closer to me than I should have. But that doesn't mean I love him. Look at how he lied to me."

"Yeah, look at that. The bastard. He had a lot of nerve, hosting a cocktail party for you and tricking you into selling four of your best pieces. You probably would rather have kept them and starved another six months, hmm? Or maybe lost your farm?"

"You think what he did was ethical?" she demanded, her cheeks flushed.

Nick shrugged. "I don't know beans about ethics when it comes to falling in love. Love turns people into raving maniacs. Just take a good look at yourself if you don't believe me."

"I am not a raving maniac!" she yelled, all but pulling her hair out by the roots.

"Don't tell me you think you've been acting rational! The guy wants to help you. Did he hold a gun to anyone's head and force them to buy your work? He isn't trying to, heaven forbid, turn you into a kept woman, is he?"

"Don't be ridiculous. We haven't even...uh, you know..." She stopped in embarrassment.

"I don't know what you're complaining about then, unless it's that you *haven't*...you know." His soft chuckle mocked her. "Come on, lighten up, Gabriella. Artists have always had patrons who supported them so they could indulge their creativity, for the simple reason that not all good artists are appreciated while they're alive. We can't all make a living at this. Until your friend came along, you were broke and facing the end of your career. Now you're not. I think maybe you ought to thank your lucky stars he happens to have a weakness for your big brown eyes."

Gabriella promptly rescinded every nice thing she'd ever thought about Nick. He was as bad as Christian, for heaven's sake! Men! They were more trouble than they were worth.

A couple of evenings later while Nick and Gaby were relaxing before the fire, she got a telephone call from Bob Turnbow, who had somehow tracked her down. The older man wondered if she would be interested in placing some of her pieces in one of the merchant booths at Christmas at Old Fort Concho, an annual event in early December that usually drew close to forty thousand visitors for three days of festivities. The town of San Angelo had grown up around the site of the frontier fort, which had been established in 1867, and some of the restored military buildings now housed a museum.

Mr. Turnbow apologized for not giving Gaby more notice, explaining that an opening had occurred when one of the regular merchants had to cancel unexpectedly. "After having seen those pieces of yours last week, I wondered if you might help us out." As if she needed to be persuaded, he added, "It will be good exposure for you."

Gaby put one hand on her hip as she stared at the telephone. "Are you sure it was your idea for me to participate?"

He seemed surprised at the question. "Whose idea did you think it was?"

She hesitated, then decided she might as well be honest. "I thought maybe Christian had suggested it."

"John Christian Lindsey?" He chuckled. "You don't think I'm sharp enough to recognize the quality of your sculpture?"

"No, that's not what I meant. I just thought he might have used his influence to get my work included."

"I see." Actually he sounded a little confused. "Well, Gabriella, let me set your mind at ease. It wasn't a question of John Christian's applying his influence here. We're willing to consider suggestions from anyone, but we don't act on those suggestions unless the products are first rate. By the same token, I wouldn't spend several thousand dollars on a piece of art just because the artist was recommended by someone I like and respect. I don't buy art just to support the artist, and I don't know anyone else who does."

The invitation might not have come from Christian, she thought wryly, but Mr. Turnbow's blunt message sounded as if it flowed straight off the pen of the illustrious editor.

A wave of intense relief surged through her. Ever since she left Bronte she'd been tormented by the thought that she shouldn't have kept the money for those four sculptures. If she hadn't been on the verge of ruin, she wouldn't have. Now she could stop feeling guilty. "Mr. Turnbow, I'd be honored to display my work at the Christmas festivities," she told him with a light heart.

On Gaby's seventh day at Marble Falls—a perfect, windless day when temperatures climbed into the upper fifties—they poured the bronze. Then on Monday, three days before Thanksgiving, they began removing the ceramic shells and dressing down the metal sculptures, grinding and smoothing over all the rough spots and seams. Nick used a welding torch to attach the pieces that couldn't be cast with the larger objects, including the Apache's lance and the pirate's cutlass.

For Nick's sake, Gabriella tried to hide her sudden restless desire to get back home. She'd told Nick upon her arrival that she would spend Thanksgiving with him, and they'd talked about going to Austin for dinner, since he didn't have any family. Even though it looked as if they'd be finished working sometime Wednesday, she simply couldn't let Nick spend the holiday alone, no matter how much she wanted to return to Bronte.

No matter how much you want to see Christian, her conscience corrected her, and Gaby didn't bother arguing the point.

Ever since Bob Turnbow had informed him that Gabriella wouldn't be back in Bronte until the weekend, Christian had been fighting the impulse to drive down to Marble Falls. He told himself it would be a wasted trip—that he was the last person she would want to see. But he was planning to spend Thursday with his father anyway; what was another eighty miles? He could swing by the foundry on Wednesday afternoon, say hello to Gaby and introduce himself to her kindly old friend Nick, then go on and spend the night in Kerrville. No sweat.

Unfortunately he got hung up at work and wasn't able to get away until five o'clock on Wednesday. Since his car was already packed and the gas tank full, he left town directly from the office. Even so, it was after dark by the time he reached the little town of Marble Falls, and then he had to stop at two gas stations before he found anyone who could tell him where Nick Jantzen lived.

The last young lady whom he asked for directions seemed to be quite well acquainted with Mr. Jantzen, and she promptly drew up a map showing the location of the foundry. As she looked Christian over, she informed him that she would be happy to escort him out to Nick's place personally. "It's kinda hard to find at night," she said with a dimpled smile. "The road twists and turns a lot up in the hills."

Christian declined her offer with thanks. Too late, he learned that she hadn't been kidding about how difficult it was to find the foundry in the dark. The rain that began suddenly and grew heavier by the minute didn't make it any easier. Several wrong turns later he finally pulled the Jag up in front of an interesting multilevel, cedar-shingled house set far back from the highway amid a grove of oak trees. The place was dark except for the glow of a hearth fire that he could see through the front windows. Nothing had ever looked so inviting as that flickering light.

According to Christian's wristwatch, it was after eight. He was tired from the long drive and disgusted at the difficulty he'd had in locating this place, and he needed a cup of coffee. More than that, he needed to see Gaby, even though she probably wouldn't be thrilled to see him.

He climbed out of the car and sloshed through the downpour toward the covered front porch. After knocking, he stood wiping the rain off his face, preparing an apology in case it was past the old man's bedtime.

A moment later two lights came on, one inside and one on the porch, and the door swung abruptly open. He found himself facing a man close to his own age, maybe an inch shorter and distinctly well built. And not bad looking,

Christian thought unhappily. This had better be just some relative visiting Jantzen, or Louise was in big trouble.

"Can I help you?" the man asked and then took a closer look at Christian.

"I hope so." Still shaking off drops of water, Christian hesitated. "I understand Nick Jantzen lives here. You aren't by any chance his grandson, are you?"

Before the man could answer, Christian heard Gaby's voice floating out from somewhere inside the house. "What is it, Nick? Hurry up, would you? It's getting cold in here."

Ten

___

The sound of her voice sent a bolt of electric excitement slamming through Christian. Lord, he'd missed that woman! Then, when Gaby's words registered, his face tightened into a mask as he stared at the man in the doorway. This muscular Adonis with all his teeth and apparently every other part of his body in perfect working order was Gaby's old friend Nick?

Christian stood motionless, torn between wanting to leave and aching to see Gaby.

After studying him with interest for a moment, the other man extended his hand. "I'm Nick Jantzen. And you're Christian. Christian Lindsey, right?"

Trying not to look as perturbed as he felt, Christian shook hands with him. "How did you know?"

Nick shrugged. "A lucky guess." He gestured with one hand. "Come on in. Gabriella will be glad to see you."

"I don't think—" Christian began, but at that moment Gaby called again, "Nick? Was someone at the door?" and wandered out to the entry hall to see for herself.

The golden glow of the firelight outlined her slim figure in jeans and red-and-white-striped sweater and her dark mane of hair. With a familiar sinking sensation in his stomach, he wanted to reach out and touch her, to thread his fingers into the tousled length of silk that framed her face and spilled over one shoulder. Her warm beauty gripped him by the heart and made it difficult for him to breathe.

Gabriella's eyes widened when they met Christian's. Besides surprise, he couldn't tell what feelings his sudden appearance had evoked in her. Was that a smile playing around the corners of her lips?

"John Christian Lindsey," she said, too softly for him to detect any anger. "What in the world are you doing here?"

He scratched one cheek, his expression closed. "I just happened to be in the neighborhood."

Gaby and Nick exchanged glances. Nick looked faintly amused, which inspired Christian with a strong urge to hit something. He turned to leave so he wouldn't. "It looks as if I came at a bad time."

She was out on the porch beside him in a second, catching his arm to stop him. "Where do you think you're going? You're soaking wet!"

He hadn't really noticed, but she was right. He looked down at the slim hand gripping his wrist and saw that her feet were bare. "Go back inside, Gaby, or you'll get wet, too."

"You can't leave until you dry off." She slid her hand down to take his. "Christian, your hand feels like ice!" She tugged at him. "Come on. You have to warm up."

"The heater in my car works fine, thanks. I still have a few miles to go tonight."

Gabriella knew a moment of terror that he was going to vanish back into the rainy night. She clenched her fingers around his larger, more powerful hand and stopped trying to act casual about this. "Please, Christian!" Looking up at him in the sallow porch light, she swallowed hard. "Come inside. I want to talk to you."

Christian wondered what she wanted to talk about. Nick? His gaze shifted to the other man, who was leaning against the door frame watching the interchange with studied innocence.

Abruptly Nick straightened. "No sense in trying to drive while it's raining. These roads aren't very safe at night under the best conditions. How about a cup of hot coffee?"

Christian capitulated, albeit without enthusiasm. As long as he'd dragged them away from whatever they were doing, he might as well find out what was going on here. At least she was wearing clothes, he thought grimly.

As if she feared he would change his mind, Gabriella kept possession of his hand until she'd brought him face-to-face with the blazing fire. Nick left the room to get the coffee. When he returned, Christian was still standing before the flames, warming his hands, while Gabriella hovered nearby, offering to take his jacket and asking if he wouldn't rather sit down. He assured her he was fine. He'd been sitting for hours.

Nick passed him the steaming mug. "Did you drive from San Angelo this evening?"

Nodding, Christian raked his fingers through his damp hair. "I'm on my way to Kerrville. The rain slowed me down."

Gaby finally persuaded him to remove his slightly sodden wool sport coat, which she draped over a footstool next to the hearth. When she turned back to him, she let her eyes linger on the breadth of his shoulders in his tailored pinstriped shirt, admiring the way his chest tapered down to a lean waist and sexy tush. When her breathing grew quick and shallow, she forced her eyes back to his face. "You're going to spend Thanksgiving with your father?"

Afraid of seeing more of those telling visual exchanges between the other two, Christian was careful to look only at the fire. "That's right."

After studying his guests a moment, Nick went to the closet and rummaged around in it. He emerged with both arms full, dropped a couple of blankets and pillows on the sofa and handed a man's overcoat to Christian. "Can I make a suggestion? Put this on, go out to your car and bring in your suitcase. The couch unfolds into a bed—not exactly the Hilton, but you should be comfortable sleeping there. There's a telephone in the kitchen if you'd like to let your father know the roads are too bad for you to go any farther tonight. And while you're getting out of those wet clothes, Gabriella can heat up some of the hot dogs left over from supper."

As if he knew Christian was about to refuse his hospitality and understood the reason for that refusal, Nick headed for the stairs. "I'm going to bed. Don't worry that you two will keep me awake, Christian." He threw a meaningful grin over his shoulder. "Gabriella's bedroom is down the hall from you there—" he pointed "—and mine is way up at the top of the house. Once I close my door, I can't hear a thing that goes on downstairs." He winked at Gabriella and took the steps two at a time.

Christian glanced down at Nick's coat and then back up at Gaby. "Was he trying to tell me something?"

Blushing, she rubbed her flattened palms down her thighs. "It sounded that way. I think he thought you might have gotten the wrong idea about us...about Nick and me."

"What kind of wrong idea?"

"Well . . . that Nick and I have something going. I don't know where you'd get an idea like that . . ."

He regarded her intently. "You mean you *don't* have something going with Nick?"

She gave him a gentle smile and a head shake and bent over the couch to rearrange the pillows and blankets. "He's a very good friend."

"Almost like an uncle?" Christian asked wryly, putting down his coffee to slide his arms into the coat sleeves.

"Considering his age, I'd say he's more like a big brother." She looked up then and smiled again when she saw what Christian was doing. He must be going to stay for the night! She abandoned the bedding and picked up Christian's nearly empty cup. "I'll get you some more coffee. Or would you rather have something else to drink with your hot dogs?"

"Whatever." He watched her start for the kitchen, his eyes serious. "I'll take whatever you want to give me."

Gabriella decided the weiners would taste better cooked over the fire, so she knelt there holding the long-handled fork toward the flames until the hot dogs were brown all over and sizzling. Meanwhile, Christian took his suitcase into the bathroom, then came back out in a white sweatshirt and khaki trousers and stretched out on the thick rug near the hearth. After Gaby had doctored up the buns with mustard, chili and pickle relish and crowned each one with a fat frankfurter, she placed a heaping plate on the floor next to him. He swore he would never be able to eat all that.

By the time he finally quit, he'd managed to put away four hot dogs and two more cups of coffee. Gaby lay on her side nearby, propped up on her elbow, watching him. "I thought you weren't hungry," she said, brown eyes sparkling.

He lay down flat on his back, stuck one forearm beneath his head and sighed. "My appetite made a remarkable recovery." After a minute of staring up at the ceiling, enjoying the blessed comfort of a warm fire and a full belly, he turned his head and met her gaze. "I wasn't sure you would let me in tonight."

Gaby supposed she should remember her hurt and outrage over Christian's behaviour, but at the moment all she could think about was how good it was to see him. She smiled. "I'm glad you came. I've missed you."

"You have?" His low voice feathered down her spine and made her shiver. The look in his hazel eyes ignited a wildfire in the most vulnerable part of her, and before she knew it, fingers of flame were shooting out from the source, racing along her nerves and heating her blood.

Gaby knew what was the matter with her, and she knew what the solution was, and from the tension around Christian's mouth and his eyes, he was experiencing the same problem. The dark hand that lay by his side was clenched, the fingers digging relentlessly into the soft pile of the rug. His body was all but sending up smoke signals.

Before she could forget that Nick was upstairs and do something more brazen and risky than she'd ever done in her entire life, Gaby scrambled to her feet and picked up Christian's empty plate. Mumbling something about cleaning things up, she vanished into the kitchen where she tried to calm down by taking out her frustration on the dirty dishes.

When she returned to the living room, Christian lay just as he had before, except that he seemed to have relaxed. His eyes were closed, but when she sat down again on the rug he opened them and focused on her with an ironic grin, as if he knew what she'd been trying to escape. There was just enough devilry in his expression to warn her that running away wouldn't do any good.

Ignoring his unspoken message, she drew one knee up and propped her chin on it. "It's occurred to me since I saw you last that I forgot to give you your bronze." His dark eyebrows rose slightly. "The bronze I promised you."

"Ahh." His eyes drifted momentarily to the fire. "You don't owe me a bronze, Gaby. After the party, you weren't feeling very charitable toward me. I understand that." Taking a deep breath, he sat up and faced her squarely. "I want to apologize for what I did. I didn't mean to offend your pride or denigrate your independence. It should have been apparent to me that you can take care of yourself."

At that point Gaby almost lost her head and told him that maybe she *had* been a little hasty in tossing all those accusations at him the night of the party, but she bit back the admission and said faintly, "I'm sure you meant well."

"Oh, yeah." Self-mockery laced his tone. "I acted with the best of intentions, and everybody knows where those lead us." He was suddenly very solemn. "I can assure you, Gaby, I'm not going to interfere anymore."

"You're not?"

He shook his head. "I know you're a strong person, and I've never doubted your talent. The thing is . . . it's hard for me to watch people hurt." His voice dropped a note. "It's even harder when I care about someone."

Her stomach fluttered crazily at the implication of his words. She thought the pounding of her heart would crack a couple of ribs when he added hoarsely, "I'd like very much to keep seeing you, Gaby. I promise, I'll keep my hands off."

"Keep your hands off what?" she asked breathlessly.

He gave her a strained smile. "Your career," he said with a glimmer of humor. "Not being a saint, I can't promise to keep my hands off anything else."

She felt suddenly like whooping for joy. "I think I can live with that risk."

Several long, hushed moments later she tore her gaze from his. He exuded a kind of magnetic appeal that was almost impossible to withstand, but she knew that, for tonight at least, she had to resist. She got up onto her knees. "I guess I'd better let you go to sleep now."

"I'd rather you stayed here and talked to me."

Talk? She could handle that. But she could tell from his face that he was tired. "What kind of shape would we be in tomorrow if I kept you up all night, Christian?"

He chuckled, sprites of mischief dancing in his eyes. "I don't know about you, but I'd be in terrific shape. Besides, after drinking three cups of coffee, I probably won't be able to sleep."

"So what do you suggest?"

"I told you—stay with me. Hold my hand, talk to me. Maybe your voice will put me to sleep."

Wait a second. Talking was one thing; holding his hand was something else entirely... something that might lead to much more than just sleep. However tempting that prospect was, she needed more time. Last week she'd been convinced Christian was all wrong for her. Now she needed to talk to him, maybe just to hold his hand, to get to know everything about him. To give her head a chance to stop spinning.

Slowly she stood up. "Are you ready for bed?" When he nodded, she moistened her lips. "Then I guess I'll wash my face and change. Do you want me to show you how to unfold the couch?"

With a perfectly straight face, he said, "I think I can figure that out all by myself, Gaby, but thank you anyway."

She dismissed his thanks with a weak smile. "If you aren't asleep when I come back, I'll consider staying with you awhile." Hastily she clarified that. "So we can talk."

Christian nodded gravely and waited until she was gone before he got to his feet.

The fire had burned down to glowing red embers and Christian was beginning to wonder if Gaby really planned to come back, when suddenly she appeared in the doorway. Although she moved carefully through the shadowy dimness, she bumped into the frame of the sofa bed and clamped a hand to her mouth to muffle her cry of pain.

He sat up. "Go ahead and scream, Gaby. I'm awake."

Moaning as quietly as possible, she rubbed her injured shin. "You may not be sleeping, but Nick is. And I don't care what he said, he'd be down here in a second if I screamed."

Did she think he needed a reminder of Nick's presence? Christian braced himself upright, leaning back on both arms, and eyed her quizzically. It was too dark to tell what she was wearing. "Come here and let me see what you've done to yourself. I'm an expert at leg injuries."

As she moved around the side of the bed and sat down next to him, she could tell that he wasn't wearing the sweatshirt anymore. She wished she could see his bare chest better, but she didn't think it would be a very good idea to turn on the light.

Reaching for her leg, he encountered the thick denim of her jeans, then touched her sleeve and fingered the soft knit of her sweater. "Do you always sleep in your street clothes?"

"I had second thoughts about putting on a nightgown." She sounded embarrassed.

He slid his hand down to her wrist, where he found the pulse point and began to stroke it with his thumb. "Don't you trust me?"

Distracted, she stammered, "I, uh, I'm not sure I trust myself."

Her honesty made him smile in the dark. "Do you feel safe in those jeans?"

Safe? She wouldn't put it that way. "I just don't feel quite so vulnerable. Except when you do *that*." She tugged at her wrist to show him what she meant.

"Sorry." He released her hand, and perversely she wished he hadn't. "How am I going to check your injury if you're wearing jeans, Gaby?"

"My leg's fine. It's stopped hurting."

"You sure?"

"Yes," she said huskily.

"Good." He lay back down. "Come on, climb in." Anticipating her shock, he added quietly, "We're just going to talk, remember? If you sit across the room, we'll have to shout. We wouldn't want to wake up Nick, now would we?"

"But . . . you want me to get in bed with you?"

If the truth were known, he wanted a lot more than that, but this would at least be a start. He reached out and ran a hand down her thigh. "Gaby, you said it yourself—you're safe in those jeans." That wasn't exactly what she'd said, and they both knew it, but he went on before she could correct him. "Just let me hold you awhile. I've been wanting to do that from the first night I saw you. I'm not going to ravish you on the sofa in Nick's living room with him just upstairs."

"You'd ravish me otherwise?" she asked ironically, halfway wishing Nick wasn't at home.

"I don't know. I might try. You wouldn't have to worry, though. You could always outrun me."

Gaby decided not to tell him she had shamefully little inclination to run from him. She stood up and pretended to be in total control of the situation. "Well, as long as I'm safe, I might as well get comfortable."

"Sure. Why not?" When he lifted the blanket, she slipped beneath it and moved cautiously into his arms. Her breath caught in her throat at his clean scent...at the delicious feel of her body coming into slow, sweet contact with his. She slid her hands around his smoothly muscled back and then down to his waist, and when her fingers discovered the supple warmth of his flesh, ten thousand volts of need quivered through her. She was reassured of her safety, but only minimally so, when she encountered the elastic band of his Jockey shorts.

Closing her eyes, she tried to ignore the alarming intensity of her desire. "You don't sleep in pajamas, hmm?" she asked in what she hoped was a normal voice.

He was silent a moment. "Actually the shorts are a concession to you. I usually don't sleep in anything at all." After another brief hesitation, he pulled back just a bit and said, "If you hand me my pants, I'll put them on. I guess I didn't think about my leg." Which wasn't exactly accurate; he'd thought long and hard about his leg, worrying about whether it would bother Gabriella, and he'd obviously made the wrong decision.

"I don't know what—" Sudden understanding struck her in the midsection like a fist, and she tightened her arms fiercely around him. "No, Christian, you're wrong!"

"It's all right, Gaby. I'm usually more careful. I just wanted to get as close to you as I could. While we talk, of course," he said teasingly.

Her eyes stung at the realization that he was trying his damnedest to put her at ease. "I want to get close to you, too," she said unsteadily. "As close as two people can get. But here in Nick's house we don't have any choice but to stick to conversation. We have no privacy here. And when I found out you weren't wearing pajamas, I knew it was going to be a lot more difficult for me to... well, to just talk." She curved her palm against his cheek and felt a muscle jumping there. "You tempt me so much it terrifies me, Christian." She swallowed. "I don't want to feel hurried or furtive. I need to be sure the time is right, and the place."

"And the person?"

"I don't think there's any question about the person."

He exhaled slowly and started to relax again. "I understand. Why don't I put on my pants?"

When he moved to sit up, she caught him by the shoulders and held him near. "No, wait, Christian. Why don't you stay right where you are and stop me if I get out of line? I'd like to be able to enjoy touching you."

He groaned. "I don't know, Gaby. The temptation is pretty potent on my end, too. Who's going to keep *me* in line?"

"Your conscience?" she said hopefully.

"I should warn you, my conscience may not be functioning too reliably tonight. It tends to short-circuit when I'm in bed with beautiful, sexy sculptresses."

She smoothed her hands down his sides and snuggled closer against him, and he felt himself drowning in a sea of pleasure that was entirely Gabriella's creation. "Don't worry, Christian," she whispered, her words tickling his ear and causing his pulse to leap. "Between us, we can handle it."

Could they? He wrapped his arms around her and held on tight, hoping for her sake that she knew what she was talking about.

Eleven

Waking early, Christian lay with just his face exposed to the cold darkness, the rest of him warm and comfortable beneath the covers. When he stirred, a pair of feminine arms tightened around his waist and a slender body cuddled closer, causing his pulse to stutter with delight. Gaby's fragrant hair brushed his cheek as she turned her head, and her lips grazed his bare throat. Her indistinct murmurs told him she was dreaming.

His heart filled up with the overwhelming certainty of his love for Gabriella Michaelson. If he outlived Methuselah, he could never get enough of just being near her...just holding her like this.

He moved cautiously to caress her and made a couple of startling discoveries in the process. The first was that sometime during the night she'd shed her sweater and jeans. His fingertips had never encountered anything so tantalizingly soft, so inviting, as her satin-textured skin. He'd never

wanted to explore anything the way he wanted to study Gaby's body. *Patience,* he cautioned himself. He had to believe their time would come, eventually.

The second discovery he made was that his left leg, the
one that ended below the knee, was sandwiched cozily between both of hers. When he tried to ease it out, the muscles of her thighs tensed and held him there. A few minutes
later he tried again, and this time she clenched her arms
around his middle and made small noises of protest. He left
his leg where it was then, thinking that it would be interesting to catch her reaction when she finally awoke.

She surprised him, though. One minute she was totally
dead to the world, and a few seconds later he felt the stiff-
ening of her body that meant she'd returned to consciousness. Her hands drifted up and down his back as she
oriented herself to his feel and his scent. But when she'd relaxed, stretching against him and changing positions
slightly, she made sure his injured leg remained between hers
with a subtle pressure that Christian felt clear to his heart.

Sleepily she kissed him good morning, and they lay talking in hushed tones for nearly an hour. Knowing how easy
it would be to get carried away, both of them carefully limited their touching. Just as daylight started slipping into the
room, she sat up and let the covers fall away from her.

He wasn't ready for the night to end. "Where are you
going?"

"To turn up the thermostat and get dressed. Nick will be
downstairs wanting breakfast before long." She glanced
down at herself, then back at him where he lay against the
pillows watching her with a sensual admiration she could
detect even in the dimness. That look of his made her feel
beautiful. In case he was wondering about her nearly naked state, she added breathlessly, "I got a little warm last
night."

"Did you?" He chuckled with quiet enjoyment. "Well, you'd better hurry up and dress, or you'll freeze that gorgeous derriere of yours."

Grinning, she headed for her bedroom. Fifteen minutes later she was back, wearing a skirt and sweater and knee boots, her hair fashioned into an intricate french braid. By then Christian had shaved and dressed, folded up the sofa bed and returned the bedding to the closet. They went into the kitchen together and had just coordinated a plan to cook bacon and eggs when the telephone on the counter jangled.

"Nick'll get that upstairs," Gaby informed Christian, then frowned at him. "Oh, dear. You never called your father to tell him you'd be late."

He began laying out strips of bacon in the skillet. "It's okay. He wasn't expecting me until today."

"What if you'd gone on to Kerrville last night?" Suspicion sparkled in her dark eyes. "Or did you ever really intend to do that?"

He did his best to look wounded. "Of course I did! Dad's place is pretty small, so I planned to stay in a motel. I had no idea your kindly old friend Nick would be so hospitable."

"My kindly old friend?" she repeated dryly. "Why does it sound as if you're quoting someone when you call him that?"

"Maybe because I *am* quoting someone...the same source who assured me Nick was old enough to be your grandfather and probably didn't have all his teeth."

Gaby laughed as she got down three plates from the cabinet. "You don't mean Louise!"

"Yep."

She shook her head. "All I can say is, she meant well, I'm sure. At least she had the essence of the situation right. She knew Nick and I are just very good friends."

"He seems like a nice guy," Christian said carefully, cracking eggs into a bowl and then starting to whip them with a fork. "I guess you two have something planned for today?"

Hearing Nick's footsteps clattering down the stairs, Gaby said hurriedly and with heartfelt regret, "Yes, we do." It was going to kill her when Christian left.

When their host appeared in the doorway, she greeted him and then said to Christian, "Nick and I are driving to Austin to eat barbecue at the Iron Works. If you weren't going to spend the day with your father, you could go with us."

Nick took a deep appreciative sniff of the bacon and coffee and patted Gaby's back as he passed her to get a clean cup. "Listen, Gabriella, I'm afraid I'm going to have to back out on that. Melinda just called and asked if I'd give her some help on one of her pieces. She's coming over about noon, and I wouldn't be surprised if we don't get through until late."

"Melinda?" Gaby asked. "She sculpts?" She had heard some of the male foundry workers comment about Nick's prettiest helper, but it had been her bright smile, not her artistic ability that had captured their attention.

"Yeah. At least she's trying to learn." He poured himself some coffee and leaned against the counter to drink it, his lazy grin daring Gaby to contradict him. Standing at the stove, Christian missed the accusatory looks Gaby was shooting at Nick.

Nick sounded penitent. "I'm sorry I have to cancel our Thanksgiving dinner plans, Gabe, but I'd really hate to put Melinda off. Up to now she's been too stubborn to let me help her, and her work is atrocious. You wouldn't want to be responsible for stymieing her creative development, would you?"

"Good heavens, no!" Gaby wished she could bop Nick over the head with the skillet for trying to arrange her love life. What made him think Christian wanted to spend the day with her?

Even with his back to them, Christian thought he understood what was going on between the other two. He waited until they'd all finished eating and cleaning up the breakfast dishes and Nick had left them alone in the living room before he asked her casually to come with him to Kerrville. "I'll have you back here tonight," he said.

She glanced away from him. "Christian, Nick's just an overgrown Cupid. He conned you into this. You aren't under any obligation to invite me for Thanksgiving dinner."

Laughing, he shook his head. "You know, I'm starting to like Nick more all the time. I don't feel obligated, and I damn sure don't feel sorry for you, if that's what you're going to say next." He regarded her intently. "I would like you to meet my father, and I'd like very much to spend the day with you."

When he looked at her like that, she wanted to spend a lifetime with him. A smile lit her eyes and she nodded.

On the drive to Kerrville, Christian told her a little more about his parents. "They'd given up on having children by the time I was born, and Dad always talked about my late arrival as if it were true Biblical miracle. Something like Abraham fathering Isaac at the age of one hundred."

"It's a wonder they didn't let you get away with murder."

He made a face. "As I think I told you before, everybody in church and half the people in town were watching every move I made. It's pretty hard to get away with *anything* under those circumstances. But I tried."

Remembering what Eleanor Cavendish had said about Christian's father, Gabriella racked her brain for a tactful way to ask him about it, but nothing occurred to her. "How long has your father been retired?"

"Four years. I think he would still be holding a church now if a heart attack hadn't forced him to quit. He goes to church every time the doors open. In fact, he preaches whenever the regular pastor is away." Christian gave a resigned shrug. "I've stopped trying to talk him out of doing that. I really believe Dad would rather drop dead in the middle of a rousing sermon than go out of this world quietly."

"You worry about his health?"

"Sure. He's seventy-three years old. But he is the way he is, and I don't have any illusions about changing him at this late date. Besides, some of the people in his church keep me informed of how he's doing. With all his friends, he's never really had to be alone since my mother died, and I always make sure he has grocery money."

Almost as soon as they arrived at the retirement community, Gaby saw what Christian meant. Within the first half hour, several people telephoned to make sure John Lindsey had a ride to church, and a couple of his neighbors stopped by his apartment to check on the tall gentleman with steel-gray hair and an old-fashioned gallantry that reminded her of her grandfather.

When the time came to leave for the Thanksgiving services, John Lindsey winked at his son. "Would it be all right if I escort Gabriella to your car? There's a lady next door that I want to impress. She thinks I'm over-the-hill."

The telephone rang again, and John moved to answer it. "I hope you don't mind if we go with him to church," Christian said quietly. "The tradition means a lot to him, and it shouldn't last more than an hour."

Gaby narrowed her eyes at him. "I don't have to be dragged by the hair to church, Christian. I'm not some uncivilized heathen, you know. I'll be glad to go." His unexpected laughter caused her to bristle. "Did I say something funny?"

"I was just remembering when you accused *me* of being uncivilized." His hazel eyes glittered with amusement as she blushed at the memory. He reached for her hand and laced their fingers together, tracing his thumb provocatively across her sensitive palm.

Gulping, she jerked her hand back as his father hung up the phone. "We'd better go soon," the older man said. "I'll fetch my coat."

When Gaby excused herself to comb her hair, Christian asked his father if he needed any money. John looked relieved. "I hate to admit it, son, but I could use some. I got your check on the first, as usual, but what with one thing and another I'm a little short."

"How much do you need?" Christian took out his wallet.

"Just a little. Whatever you can spare. I really don't need much."

Christian wrote out a check, knowing from his father's choice of words that John was broke. "What was it this time?" he asked, his tone devoid of censure.

"There's a family down the street that's having a hard time. The man's out of work, the wife died two years ago, the kids are sick. I do what I can. You know how it is."

Christian nodded, watching John with wry affection. As he had told Gaby, his father wasn't going to change. A moment later when she announced she was ready to go, he turned to her with an easy smile, not realizing she'd overheard most of the brief conversation.

After the church service, as they made their way through the crowd back to the car, she witnessed another interchange that shed a little more light on John Lindsey's character. A man in the congregation approached the retired minister and said, "John, Mrs. Bailey told me about the shoes you bought her children. That was a fine thing to do for them."

While John was looking uncomfortable and trying to change the subject, Gaby studied Christian, who seemed neither upset nor surprised. The money he sent his father to live on every month evidently enabled the older man to act as benevolent patron of the underprivileged. How did Christian feel about that... and what had Christian's childhood been like if his father habitually gave away the grocery money to care for everyone else?

Back in the car, when Christian asked John where he would like to go for dinner, his father informed them that he'd received half a dozen invitations to Thanksgiving dinner in the homes of his friends. His guests would certainly have been welcome, he said, but he thought they should eat at the retirement center instead. "Some of those folks don't have anywhere to go or any family to visit them."

The dinner was thoroughly enjoyable, from the customary turkey and dressing, to the company of the old people who shared the meal. They all seemed delighted by the few visitors in their midst, expressing particular interest in Christian and Gabriella when they discovered the strikingly attractive young couple weren't married. From the questions they asked, it was clear that everyone loved the idea of a blooming romance.

After dinner, while John was resting, Christian and Gaby went out and bought a supply of staples to fill John's nearly bare pantry. Gaby couldn't help wondering how long it would be before John had depleted his stock of food again by doling it out to the poor.

When they'd said their goodbyes and were driving back to Marble Falls, Gaby turned to Christian. "Thank you for bringing me today. I enjoyed meeting your father. I like him."

"I'm glad. Thanks to you, he now admires my taste in women. And I wanted you to understand him. Dad's...well, you saw for yourself how he is."

"He seems to inspire tremendous loyalty among his friends." So did his son, for that matter.

Christian nodded, then sighed rather tiredly. "He's never been very good with money."

"Some of us have that problem," she said. "How long has he been so...so generous?"

"At least as long as I've been around. He took the commandment to 'feed my sheep' literally."

A painful lump was beginning to form in her throat. It was obvious that John Lindsey was as saintly as they come, but she couldn't help but be concerned for the welfare of the boy Christian had been. "And did he feed you? When you were growing up, did you always have enough to eat?"

"Most of the time." Seeing her stricken expression, he grinned crookedly. "To a rebellious youth, even *one* missed meal is enough to cause the feeling that the world's against you. But tell me, Gabriella, do I look as if I've suffered?"

No. He was the picture of good health, with his hard muscular length, his dark skin, his thick glossy hair and warm eyes. But that didn't matter. Just the thought of Christian's having done without something he needed was enough to squeeze all the joy out of her heart and make her feel like weeping.

When Christian saw her tears, he wanted to grab her and shake her. She could cry over his nonexistent misfortunes, he thought with sudden bitterness, but she would rather starve than let him help her out of her own financial difficulties. It was totally illogical, and unfair as well. Even though he'd agreed not to help anymore with her career, he still felt frustrated, cheated. Because of his leg, he'd been forced to lean on others more than he liked. Why couldn't Gaby do a little of the same? Surely their relationship should accommodate some give and take on both sides!

He spoke a bit more roughly than usual. "My childhood was all right, Gabriella. Most of my problems I brought on myself, so don't blame my father for the way I turned out."

"I hadn't noticed anything wrong with the way you turned out."

"What about my annoying tendency to stick my nose in your business?"

She hoped her teasing smile would diffuse his tension. "Ah, but you haven't done that for almost twenty-four hours. That's a record, isn't it?"

He exhaled raggedly. "I promised I wouldn't interfere, and I'll keep my word. You don't have to keep reminding me."

"But . . . but *you* mentioned it, I didn't. I'm not worried about it." In truth, she was starting to wish she hadn't been so adamant about it in the first place. She would have liked to ask Christian's opinion on which pieces to display at the Fort Concho Christmas celebration. But she couldn't bring it up without looking like a fool.

"Okay," he snapped. "I mentioned it. It won't happen again. Could we please talk about something else?"

Concern over his father must have made him out of sorts, she figured. She kept the conversation light and pleasant the rest of the way back to the foundry, and Christian's mood had improved by the time they arrived.

Nick's truck was gone, and Nick himself was nowhere to be seen. "He and Melinda have probably gone out to eat," Gaby guessed, looking in the refrigerator. "It seems the best I can offer you is a bologna-and-cheese sandwich."

"After everything we ate at noon, a sandwich will be plenty," Christian said. "I really need to head back to San Angelo." Much as he hated to leave, he was scheduled to take part in the official opening of the shelter for the homeless the next day, and he needed to get some work done at the office, too.

An hour later when she walked him out to his car, he drew her slowly into an embrace that kindled a scorching fire of need inside him. He hoped it wasn't too obvious what all these unfulfilled goodbyes and weeks of tormenting abstinence were doing to him.

"When will I see you again?" he asked hoarsely, his mouth buried in her hair, his senses glorying in her enticing perfume and her silky softness.

With galloping pulse, she leaned against him, a sweet throbbing deep inside making her achingly aware of her femininity. She caressed his back distractedly, conveying her desperate wish to keep him here. She could barely speak. "I'm driving back home tomorrow."

"Would you please let me pick you up in Bronte tomorrow evening for the weekend?"

Spend the weekend with him? Dear Lord, she wanted to!

"Please, Gaby."

She felt as though she'd been subconsciously getting ready for this from the first night she met Christian. Lifting her face, she kissed him, and the moment her hungry lips touched his, he had his answer.

Twelve

—

Upon arriving home the next day, the first thing Gabriella did was take out the bronze pirate and put him on the sculpting stand where she could admire him as she finished unpacking. There was no question about it, this was the best thing she'd ever done. Louise, when she brought over Gabriella's bank deposit slip, seconded that opinion.

When Christian came to pick her up that evening, Gaby told him to look around to see which bronze he wanted. His eyes, devouring the shelves of her work, veered over to the pirate, and he approached the sculpting stand with a stunned expression on his face. "Lord, Gaby...no wonder Nick knew who I was before I told him."

"Do you want him? I cast two pirates, and you're welcome to have one of them."

"I don't know. He looks so much like me, it's a little eerie." He gave the pirate one final appraising glance and then picked up her bag. "I'll have to think it over and let you know. I've been admiring that Comanche chieftain for a long time.''

His answer surprised Gaby, because she knew just how good the pirate was. But then she also knew that Christian wasn't hung up on his own image. It was possible that he didn't realize the extent of his own good looks.

Once they reached San Angelo, they drove first to Christian's house to drop off her suitcase, then went out to Dos Amigos for Mexican food. When he asked her whether she wanted to go to a show or to one of the clubs in town that featured live bands, she executed a perfectly timed yawn and said she didn't think she could stay awake.

"Maybe I'd better take you home and put you to bed," he said, watching her. Even if she had tried, she couldn't have hidden the anticipation that flared in her eyes at his words.

When they'd first stopped by the house, he had left her things in the living room. Upon their return after supper, he glanced at her bag and attempted a joke despite the fact that his heart was trying to pound its way out of his chest. "Your room or mine?"

Gaby didn't hesitate. She wanted Christian to love her tonight. She wanted to love every sexy inch of him back. "Yours."

If he could have, Christian would have made everything perfect for Gaby, starting with his own body. Since that was out of the question, he did the best he could. He'd ordered roses from the florist and asked his housekeeper to arrange them when she came that day to clean. The mixed array of crimson and ivory blooms graced the table next to Christian's big bed, its fragrance captivating Gaby as soon as she stepped into his bedroom.

"Oh, Christian, they're beautiful!" She touched a fingertip to one blossom and inhaled deeply.

"So are you." He placed her bag on the cedar chest along one wall.

She turned and saw the raised hot tub, a gleaming brown Jacuzzi in its own alcove, banked by a junglelike growth of tropical plants and securely shuttered floor to ceiling windows. The water that bubbled in the tub looked luxuriously inviting to Gaby. She smiled. "I'll bet I know where you spend your evenings."

"Mmm-hmm. It's a great muscle relaxant. I have to be careful not to fall asleep in there." He leaned over and dipped one hand in the water to test the temperature. The stretching gesture made the fabric of his clothes hug his broad shoulders and tautly muscled thighs and sent a sharp pang of hunger lancing through Gaby. When he looked up, shaking his hand to dry it, and caught her staring at him with unguarded longing, his hazel eyes turned smoky. "There's nothing quite like sharing a whirlpool with someone... special."

Suddenly nervous, he wiped his hand on his pants leg. He'd almost said *someone you love*, and that wasn't something he wanted to lay on Gaby yet.

She arched an eyebrow. "I presume you're speaking from experience?"

"No, strictly from hearsay." It was true he'd shared the tub, but never with anyone who mattered the way Gaby did. "Would you be interested in helping me put that rumor to the test?"

"I'd be glad to, except that I didn't bring a swimsuit."

"No problem. The management of this particular establishment doesn't require swimsuits. Actually, it's a well-known fact that bathing suits just get in the way."

"Hmm... I see. Well, in that case, I guess I'm all set." She opened her suitcase to get her blue robe, then headed for the bathroom. At the door she paused and turned back. "I'd better warn you, I'm a little modest. Will you close your eyes if I ask you to?"

His eyes were warm, his smile self-mocking. "Sure, Gaby, if that's what you want. I understand all about modesty."

Gabriella undressed with trembling fingers, secured her hair back in a long, thick ponytail, then wrapped herself in powder-blue satin and emerged from the bathroom. Although the overhead light had been turned off, there were still several lamps on in the bedroom—plenty of light for her to see Christian where he waited for her in the alcove, sitting on one of the carpeted steps that led up to the Jacuzzi. She saw in one swift glance that he wasn't wearing anything, and the sight made her stomach flip over. His lean, dark-skinned beauty had never appealed to her more than at that moment when he turned his head to look at her.

Placing one hand on the rim of the tub, he stood up and balanced on his right foot. Gaby saw his proud manhood then, and a million volts of galvanic energy rocketed straight through her. She lifted both arms, begging his embrace, and only when he reached out with his free hand did she realize that she would have to go to him.

A combined imp of playfulness and passion prodded her to cross the room slowly, untying the sash on her robe as she went and then letting the satin garment come apart and slither off her arms, down to the plush white carpet. She halted two steps away from Christian and waited.

Dry-mouthed, he stared at the naked nymph who stood before him. His heart was thundering, his knee threatening to buckle, and a delicious fire seemed to be circulating through his bloodstream. He'd never seen anything as enchanting as the lush ripeness of her small perfect breasts, her honey-tinted skin, her slender shapeliness and long legs. His stunned gaze ran down her length, paused to contemplate the dark and alluring triangle at the juncture of her thighs and then lifted once more to meet her eyes. "Oh, Gaby, you really are beautiful!" He shook his head in awe and added with husky humor, "And here I was worrying that modesty was going to be a problem."

"It usually is." She opened both palms to him in a gesture that said she couldn't explain what had come over her. "I thought *you* were going to be the shy, retiring type."

In the years since his injury and rehabilitation, Christian had led an active life, swimming, skiing, wearing shorts in public from time to time...and there had been women, although none that made him forget the rest of the world the way Gabriella did. She was the first to make him wonder how he could possibly cope if she found him lacking.

He bent his head to stare down at the damaged end of his leg, then looked back up, straight into her eyes. "I don't want to have to hide from you, Gaby. I can't change the way I look."

When she saw his vulnerability to her, a wave of incredible tenderness swelled up inside her, urging her forward the final two steps. Reaching up, she framed his face with both hands. "I love the way you look, Christian. I don't want to change anything about you."

He swallowed the tightness in his throat and managed a faint smile. "On that note, maybe we should retire to the Jacuzzi?"

They sat on the side and slid down into the whirlpool, and the churning action of the heated water began at once to ease tension they hadn't even been aware of. Within minutes Gabriella felt buoyant, totally released from her inhibitions. She stretched out in sumptuous, submerged comfort, watching Christian, who had settled on the reclining seat that was molded into the shell of the spa. The water rippling over her highly sensitized nipples made her shiver. "Mmm...this feels marvelous!"

He nodded in complete agreement with her. He lay back and, through half closed eyes, studied the delectable picture Gaby made with the rosy peaks of her breasts occasionally peeking above the surface of the water as if to flirt with him. His loins filled rapidly with a heat that had nothing to do with the water temperature.

When Christian's eyes began to smolder, Gaby ran her tongue over her lips. "Is that seat comfortable?"

"Absolutely." His smile was slow, seductive. "Come over here and I'll show you."

She didn't wait for another invitation. Gliding over to him, she supported herself with her hands on the smooth edge of the seat and bobbed up and down a little in the water while he lay there ravishing her with his beautiful eyes, his breathing ragged. She thought she knew what was happening to him, because her own body signals seemed to be in upheaval . . . a sensually exhilarating chaos.

"Here I am," she announced.

"Yes." The word came out hoarsely. He reached for her and caught her shoulders, gripping her with strong hands and lifting her at the same time that he leaned toward her. His mouth met hers in a kiss so shockingly potent it singed her clear down to her toes. His silky lips caressed hers, and his tongue probed, seeking and then answering her deepest needs. The kiss went on and on, drawing them closer together until her bare skin was mercilessly crushed against the hair-dusted plane of his torso.

With a sudden groan, he lifted her all the way up onto his lap and wrapped her in his arms. He buried his face against her throat and ran his hands up and down her slender sides, tracing the shape of her breasts with his thumbs and, without even touching the nipples, causing them to harden.

She felt a geyser of water pulsing against her sensitive skin, felt the pressure of Christian's aroused sex beneath her and moaned. "You weren't kidding about the seat being comfortable, were you?" She wove her fingers into his hair, conveying a sense of desperation. "Are you sure it's legal for a hot tub to be this stimulating?"

He tried to laugh, but the sound caught somewhere in his chest and he ended up raising his head for air. Taking advantage of his relaxed grasp, Gaby turned on his lap so her legs straddled his. She pushed him back down against the recliner and lifted herself above him until her breasts were level with his mouth. As she ran her hands across the damp brown skin of his shoulders, she felt him take one nipple into his mouth and begin to tease it with light tongue strokes. A thousand vivid sensations of pleasure spiraled through her, causing her to clutch his head and press his face against her breasts.

Although Gabriella was the sweetest, sexiest water sprite he'd ever been lucky enough to get naked and romp with, Christian didn't think he could sit still for much more of her wriggling enticement. Grasping her gently, he eased her off just a bit and regarded her with eyes shaded green with emotion. "Gaby, don't think I'm not enjoying this, because I am. Believe me, I am! But it's killing me!" When her dark eyes widened and she started to move, he held her firmly where she was. "I don't want you to go, angel. I need more, not less."

Relieved, she melted down against him.

"You need more?" Her mouth curved into a hopeful smile against his heaving chest.

"I need to love you. *Now*."

She turned her face and touched the moist tip of her tongue to one of the small, flat, coppery nipples that were so endearingly masculine. Trailing her tongue upward, she located the erratic pulse just below his jawline and nuzzled there before moving on to his ear. "I've wanted to love you for weeks," she confessed in a whisper.

Beneath the water, he explored her silky skin, roaming up and down her back, cupping the nape of her neck and the curve of her hip as he fought for inner control over his rising passion. He still wasn't sure he should be doing this. "Gaby... is the time right now? The place? Are you really ready for this? And are you sure it's safe for you?"

She answered the questions in the order that he'd asked them: "Yes, yes, yes!" Each time she spoke—each time she took a breath—her breasts grazed his chest and made her almost painfully aware of her need to become a part of him, to make him a part of her. "Yes, it's safe. You don't have to worry about that."

Christian gave her a long, searching look and saw that she wanted this as much as he did. Finally convinced, he put his hands on her waist and shifted her over, and within seconds they had switched places. It only took a moment to fit them together the way he'd been dreaming about. As she accepted his throbbing strength, he shut his eyes and expelled his breath in sharp satisfaction. He felt her fingers clutching at him, stroking his back and then his hips and the flexing length of his thighs. When he moved inside her, he felt her silken muscles tighten to hold him. Vibrantly erotic sensations sang along his nerves and the blood raced hot and rich through his veins. Every part of his body, every cell, every last pore, was more alert and alive and receptive to feeling than it had ever been before.

A powerful need gripped Gaby—the need to touch Christian, to learn his unique shape and feel with her fingertips. As he filled her and moved subtly against her, whispering endearments and groaning her name, she smoothed her hands over his supple flesh, relishing his rough male texture and his lean muscularity. She caressed each part of him that she could reach and felt her heart soar as they improvised their own special steps in the age-old dance of love.

Enveloped in water, the two of them were weightless, warm, deliciously clean, tuned in to feelings more intensely provocative than either had ever experienced.

A moment later, a single thrust later, Christian felt a rocket blast off...felt several tons of dynamite torpedo through him and rip him apart in the most pleasantly shattering explosion he'd ever imagined. Beneath him, Gaby was holding on to him, laughing or crying, he couldn't tell which, and murmuring something about how good it was...how very, very good he felt.

"Mmm, Christian...don't move. Stay right here."

Compliantly he sank down in the water and lay there on top of her, blissfully contented, more certain than ever that he wanted to spend the rest of his life with this lady.

How they'd fallen asleep, Gaby would never be able to figure out. She was almost completely underwater, and the position he was in, Christian couldn't possibly have been comfortable. But they *had* dozed off, and the Lord only knew how much later it was when they finally woke up and managed to drag themselves out of the hot tub and wrap up in bath sheets, their fingers and toes all wrinkled.

Once in bed, Christian had the brilliant idea of examining Gaby to be sure the prolonged soaking hadn't caused permanent damage to her body. She thought his concern was a bit excessive, but after his slow and thorough inspection, which required that he touch her all over with infinitely gentle fingers, and sometimes even with his lips, she changed her mind and announced that she should examine him, too. "Just to be on the safe side," she said prudently.

He agreed with hardly any coaxing. In the next two hours, Gaby discovered all his secret ticklish places and the spot behind his right knee that reduced him to begging when she kissed it. She also learned that he sometimes had pain in the foot that wasn't there, and she kissed his left knee, too, so he would know she found him perfect just the way he was. Propped up on one elbow to study him as she traced the tip of her finger from his collarbone to his flat belly, she decided he resembled a broken sculpture by one of the masters, no less beautiful for being flawed.

It proved impossible to tolerate Gaby's languorous inspection without reacting, and after a while Christian's heated reactions seemed to require active participation from both of them. They made love again, and sometime before dawn yet again, and each time was more exquisitely gratifying than the last.

Saturday morning they slept late to make up for all the sleep they didn't get in the middle of the night, and then they ate a leisurely breakfast and talked about spending the afternoon in the Jacuzzi. Christian expressed some doubt that his heart would survive such a workout, so they opted for a less strenuous sport. He took her to a neighborhood court for a game of tennis and handily beat Gaby, who hadn't picked up a tennis racket in three years.

"I was awful, wasn't I?" she moaned, plopping down in exhaustion alongside the court.

He tactfully refrained from answering her question. "Why did you agree to play, Gaby? We could have found something else to do."

"I didn't think you'd be so good!"

"You didn't?" Grinning, he sat down beside her. "Why not? You mean because of this?" He flicked a hand at his artificial foot, then asked mockingly, "Didn't the noto-

rious grapevine tell you I was a hot contender for the intra-
mural doubles championship at Texas Tech one year?''

"No!" Her eyebrows drew together. "Is that true?" She
looked as if she didn't know whether to be impressed at his
skill or annoyed that no one had forewarned her.

"Sure. And before you faint from the shock of it, you
should know that while I was in school there, the place-
kicker on the varsity football team happened to be another
guy with one leg."

"You're kidding!"

He shook his head. "I am not. He made frequent head-
lines, kicking more than his share of winning Tech field
goals with his plastic foot."

"That's amazing, isn't it?"

Christian reached out and caught a strand of her dark
hair, then fingered it lazily. "I don't know about amazing,
but I'll admit it's not the norm." He tugged at the lock of
hair until she turned her head a fraction of an inch, and then
he kissed her.

Gaby felt the remainder of her depleted physical strength
seep out of her pores and melt into the grass beneath her.
She wanted to lie there forever in the bright cool sunshine
with his lips working their heart-tugging magic on hers.

After a while he raised his head and gazed down into her
eyes with warmth and feeling. "I like having you here, Gabriella Michaelson."

"I'm having a nice time." Good grief, that sounded as if
she were writing him a postcard from Disneyland! "What I
mean to say is . . ."

What I mean to say is, I love you.

In a sudden panic, she asked herself where those words
had come from. But deep inside she knew—they'd originated in her heart, and they were true. What she'd been

starting to suspect for weeks, she now knew for a fact. She loved Christian Lindsey.

Well, true or not, she couldn't blurt out such news here, when she was tired and sweaty and too confused to think.

A bit lamely, she paraphrased his words. "What I mean to say is, I like being here."

He noticed her pause but didn't comment on it. "Do you think you could come back again next weekend? There's a big Christmas shindig at Fort Concho that you should see."

Gaby took a deep breath. She'd been waiting for a chance to tell him about this. "I thought you might already know ... I've been asked to display some of my work in a merchant booth at the Fort Concho Christmas festival. Bob Turnbow called to invite me while I was at Nick's."

"Did he?" Christian kept his expression carefully neutral. "So you will come? You'll spend the weekend again?"

"Well...sure. I'd like that, if you want me to." She hoped for some further remark about her participation in the festival, and when he kept silent, she said, "Mr. Turnbow thinks the exposure will be good for my career."

To her disappointment, he just said, "I guess Bob should know about that," and then asked her what she would like for dinner.

He kept the subject off her work the rest of the day and on Sunday as well, although they talked about everything else under the sun. The more their intimate friendship grew, the more clear it became to Gaby that in matters pertaining to her career, she was on her own.

Why did she suddenly feel so let down? She had a healthy bank balance for once, she could pay the taxes and she had the prospect of making more sales next weekend. Why this irrational urge to share every detail of her life with Christian? By nature she'd always been independent. What was happening to her?

Just remember, she told herself, this crazy urge would pass. She'd vowed to prove to her father that Gabriella Michaelson was talented enough to succeed on her own. It wasn't necessary that she talk everything over with Christian, even if he *did* happen to be the most wonderful man she'd ever met.

Anyway, she admitted, feeling strangely lost, he didn't seem to be interested in her career anymore.

Thirteen

Gabriella's worries about her relationship with Christian didn't miraculously go away. If anything, they grew worse as the week passed. She was beginning to feel as if her pride had backed her into a corner, and it was pride that kept her there, smiling and acting delighted that people were suddenly so crazy about her sculpture, when what she really wanted was for one person—Christian—to show a little enthusiasm. How could she tell him she'd been a fool from the very beginning? What would he say to such a confession?

Since the committee in charge of Christmas At Old Fort Concho wanted all the merchant booths ready by Thursday afternoon, Gabriella loaded a dozen of her bronzes into her car and drove to San Angelo on Wednesday. Christian seemed pleased to have her there all to himself that evening, and she drifted off to sleep thinking that at least there was nothing wrong with their love life.

On Thursday she checked in at the stone headquarters building and received directions to the appropriate officer's quarters where she was to share space with an antique dealer, a quilting artisan, a bookseller and a candlemaker.

"I wish we'd known you were available for this last year, Gabriella," Mrs. Conklin, the committee chairperson, said when she came around to inspect the displays.

"I wish you had, too," Gaby said with a rueful grin. "This is exactly the kind of exposure I need."

The woman bent for a closer look at the pirate. "Is this John Christian Lindsey? It is!" Her voice rose in excitement. "For heaven's sake, this is...it's simply magnificent!"

That was just the first of many such comments on Gabriella's pieces, especially the pirate. On Friday evening when Christian wandered up to the table, looking debonair and breathtakingly handsome in dark suit and red silk tie, Gaby slipped through the crowd of browsers to his side. "I want you to know you were responsible for nearly causing a riot in here a few minutes ago."

Raising one eyebrow, he crossed his arms. "In case you didn't notice, I just came in, Gaby. How could I have nearly caused a riot?"

"By looking so much like a sexy Long John Silver that half the women shoppers want to own your likeness." She gestured at the pirate. "I've had people inquiring about him ever since the doors opened at four o'clock. Half an hour ago I thought for sure two ladies were going to knock each other down trying to grab him."

"No kidding?" He eyed the bronze dubiously. "Well, I see you haven't sold him."

"I'm still waiting to see if you want him. But," she said on a triumphant note, "I took an order from a man whose girlfriend is a Robert Louis Stevenson buff. He wants to give her a copy of Long John for Christmas. I have the deposit check right here.'' She patted the pocket of her floor-length red wool skirt. Her white silk ruffled blouse emphasized the darkness of her coloring and her long curling hair and made her look like an old-fashioned china doll. Christian wished they were alone, preferably at his house...preferably in bed, so he could explore her fragility with his fingertips.

"That's nice.'' He sounded preoccupied. "Gaby, can't you get away from here for a while so we can go look at everything?''

Regretfully she shook her head. "Someone has to be here in case a visitor stops to ask questions. Louise volunteered to tend the shop for a while tomorrow afternoon so you and I can watch the variety shows and the Fort Concho Christmas Carol Pageant, but that doesn't help us much today, does it?''

Running his hand through his hair, he sighed. "Ahh, Gaby, that reminds me. I found out this afternoon that I have to go to Big Spring tomorrow. I'll probably be gone all day.'' Trey Lang had just flown to town from his home in New York, to finalize the deal with the Big Spring newspaper. As Christian had lain much of the groundwork, it made sense for him to be involved.

Swallowing her disappointment, she managed a smile. "Don't worry about it. I don't really need to see the pageant. Maybe we can catch it next year.''

"Well, you at least need to eat. If you don't come with me now, you'll probably starve to death.''

His dark prediction caused the bookseller at the next table to burst out laughing. "You go on and eat with Long John, Gabriella. We can't have you starving to death!'' The woman motioned toward the door. "I'll be glad to watch your display while you're gone.''

Christian's smile was like the sun emerging from behind a cloud. "We accept, thank you!"

"Gosh, Bitsy, you've already got your hands full," Gaby said, but Bitsy insisted.

"You can do the same for me at some point in the next three days."

Just as they were leaving the building, they ran into Judy and Jay Templeton. The tall, prematurely balding physician punched Christian's arm lightly and said, "Hey, friend, we've been looking for you two. We're on our way to eat at The Grubstake. You guys come with us."

They ended up at a picnic table, drinking beer and eating Texas stew and beans that had the delicious flavor of food prepared over an open campfire. The cooks wore authentic cowboy garb, and many of the people wandering around the fort were dressed in quaint attire of the 1870s and 1880s— U.S. cavalry uniforms, colorful Czechoslovakian and Mexican dance costumes, long calico skirts and bonnets and gaudy taffeta saloon dresses.

After they finished eating, Judy herded them around to see the other displays, particularly the buildings devoted to the customs of the French, Germans, Czechs, and Mexicans who'd played a role in the settlement of the San Angelo–Fort Concho area.

Although fascinated, Gabriella soon decided she ought to get back to her booth in order to relieve Bitsy. There, Judy exclaimed over the new pieces of Gabriella's work. "Jay," she announced, "I want this pirate. He's beautiful!"

"No way," her husband said good-naturedly. "You already compare everything I do to the way my best friend does it. You think I want a sculpture of him on my mantel, reminding me that he's perfect?"

"Perfect?" Christian picked up the pirate and held him at eye level where the peg leg could hardly be overlooked. "Not quite."

"Aww...your leg." Jay snorted. "You should complain! At least you still have all your hair."

Bitsy interrupted the laughter to inform Gabriella that a lady had come in asking for her by name while she was at supper. "She left her card and said she'd be back to talk to you tomorrow."

The business card belonged to Maxine Presswell who had a San Antonio address and telephone number. "From the way she conducted herself, I'd say she's either a gallery owner or a collector," Bitsy said.

Gaby was flattered in spite of herself. "Actually Maxine Presswell is an agent, an artist's representative. I've heard of her. She doesn't agree to represent just anybody."

"That sounds promising," Jay said. "What do you think, Christian?"

Christian's response left a lot to be desired, Gaby thought. He murmured a monosyllabic agreement and then pointed across the room, dragging Jay off a moment later to show him something that had evidently caught Christian's eye at the candlemaker's display.

Gaby told herself it was crazy to mind, but the hurt bubbled up inside her. This could be very good news for her, indeed, but he apparently wasn't even listening!

"What's the matter with him?" Judy asked in surprise.

"He's probably got something else on his mind," Gaby said with an inner sigh. Considering the way she'd responded to his help in the past, she was hardly in a position to complain about Christian's lack of support.

She almost expected Christian to vanish before the shops closed at nine o'clock, but he stuck around. As he was walking her out to the car, Bob Turnbow hailed them from a distance and joined them, clearly excited. "Gabriella, you'll never believe what's happened. I've been approached by a man who's interested in making a tax deductible gift to the city of San Angelo. One idea he's favoring is a piece of sculpture. A *large* sculpture."

Laughing, she shook her head. "Wait a minute, Mr. Turnbow. I've been through all this before, remember? Why don't you save us both a lot of trouble and suggest that he support the shelter?"

"He already has plans to make a substantial gift to the shelter fund, and he prefers to diversify his good deeds. Evidently he followed quite closely the debate over sculpture versus shelter and has seen the proposals that were submitted to the city council. Needless to say, he likes yours. That is, he likes your style. He wants you to work up another couple of ideas for him to consider." Bob grinned at her. "So you see, young lady, you may land that big commission yet!"

Suddenly she didn't know what to say. "Mr. Turnbow, that's incredible!"

"Isn't it? The thing is, he has to have your ideas on paper by noon Sunday." Hearing her indrawn breath, he chuckled. "I know. Impossible. But he won't be in town long. And he does have the wherewithal. If we can't offer him an option that he likes, he may decide to take his tax deduction elsewhere."

Within the space of one evening a prominent agent had expressed an interest in her work and now this! It almost boggled the mind. Gabriella wished Christian would say something, but he just stood there beside her, his hands in his pockets and his eyes scanning the departing crowd. "Does Maxine Presswell have anything to do with this unexpected offer?" she asked, and saw Bob's quick, inadvertent glance at Christian. Now what did that mean?

"Maxine Presswell?" Bob sounded uncomfortable. "She's in town, isn't she? I had a call from her earlier today. But to answer your question, no, she has no connection with this philanthropist."

"So who is he, anyway?"

"Now there's the hitch. He insists on remaining anonymous. He's really a rather unassuming, modest kind of fellow."

Gaby gazed at Christian, thinking that description could fit him. A sudden suspicion struck her. She slanted one more hasty look at him and said, "I can't believe this gentleman would choose my work on the basis of a proposal without actually seeing a completed bronze."

"You're absolutely right about that," Bob said. "From things he said, I gather he's familiar with your work from previous shows." He glanced at his watch. "Well, Gabriella, do you think you can complete some sketches for our generous friend by Sunday noon?"

Her lips curved. So Christian wasn't going to try to help her career anymore, hmm? "Yes, Bob, I think I can." The handsome, sneaky devil really thought he was fooling her! But where would he get that kind of money?

Once they reached Christian's house, Gaby gave him plenty of opportunity to mention the so-called anonymous donor, but instead he enticed her into the Jacuzzi. He didn't say a word about sculpture as he made love to her in the bubbling depths of the water with a hungry passion that he made no effort to hide. His potent magic made her soar when he touched her in secret places no one had ever known before and filled her with his hard warm strength. He drew her with him beyond ecstasy to a realm where she touched the moon and ten million stars ... where she experienced firsthand all the wonders of the universe.

Afterward, when they lay on the molded seat of the spa, sated and comfortable, he kissed her behind the ear and whispered, "I'm sorry I have to be gone tomorrow. I'll miss you."

"Me, too." She ran one palm down his supple chest. "But I'll probably be busy trying to come up with ideas to please this mystery benefactor."

When Christian didn't say anything, Gaby could no longer hide her knowing grin. "Are you determined to keep up this pretense, John Christian Lindsey?"

"What pretense?"

"That you don't know anything about this person who's offering to give me the commission."

He sat up and lifted one dark eyebrow. "You think I know something about him?"

"I think you more than know about him. I think you *are* him." The cool amusement that took over his expression brought a peculiar feeling to the pit of her stomach...a feeling of serious doubt. "Aren't you?"

His mouth twisted with irony, and he withdrew his hands from her naked skin. "I'm not exactly a millionaire, Gaby."

"I know that, but you wouldn't have to have a million dollars to donate a sculpture to San Angelo. Just ten or fifteen thousand." Knowing Christian, he would give his last dime for a good cause.

He glided across the hot tub to the steps and stayed there, one arm hooked over the side. "I'm sorry to disappoint you, but if I had that much money lying around just waiting to be earmarked for charity, I certainly wouldn't commission a sculpture. I'd give it all to the shelter for the homeless. One of the grants we applied for has been approved, but I don't want to see Tilly Mitchell and all the rest of those folks back out on the streets when the money runs out."

Reaching for his towel, he stood and wrapped the terry cloth bath sheet around his middle, then sat on the rim of the tub and looked at her levelly while her heart took a nosedive into despair. "You see, Michaelson, you're in luck. I'm not the anonymous benefactor. I had nothing to do with this offer. So you can go ahead and take the commission and not worry about whether I'm still trying to manipulate your career." He smiled with a trace of bitterness. "It's pretty obvious you didn't think I'd keep my word about that."

Gaby figured she had just made the biggest blunder of her life. When she lay in bed next to Christian later, neither of them touching, she fought back the tears and the words of apology that kept surfacing inside her. She wanted to tell him how wrong she'd been to think she had to make it on her own. She wanted to beg Christian to care about her work again...to talk to her about Maxine Presswell and this sculpture commission and all the decisions she wasn't equipped to make without the guidance of someone who had her best interest at heart.

But it was useless. She'd already thrown his kindness back in his face once too often.

She lay awake for hours, berating herself for screwing things up so royally and aching over the realization that no matter how beautiful it was with him, no matter how gloriously fulfilling the sex, it wasn't enough. It would never be enough for him just to offer her friendship and crave her body. She loved all of him—his unique pirate's body, yes, but also his mind, his spirit, his very heart.

She loved him for the editorials he wrote and the projects he supported. She loved him for knowing Tilly Mitchell by name. She wanted to be part of and hear about everything he cared about. The trouble was, if he had ever started to love her that way, she'd killed the love before it had a chance to take root and flourish. Out of stupid pride, she'd restricted his role in her life, and it wasn't turning out at all the way she had expected.

Christian was supposed to pick up Trey at the Sheraton at seven on Saturday morning. After getting dressed very quietly and having breakfast, he came back into the bedroom and watched Gaby sleep for a few minutes. She looked so young and soft, so touchable. But she was tough—tougher than he'd thought at first—and independent. She was determined to succeed entirely on her own. *Damn!* His hands clenched into fists as he reminded himself not to touch her.

All the way to Big Spring he could think of little except that Gaby's pride was a formidable obstacle to their future happiness. Was he willing to remain shut out of a major part of her life? He thought not. He wasn't sure how much longer he could go on this way...even if the alternative was to drop out of her life completely.

"Something on your mind?" Trey asked after seventy miles of Christian's silence. "You having problems at the paper?"

Christian glanced at the other man. Trey was in his mid-forties, blond and attractive, sophisticated and yet still comfortable among his friends from San Angelo after twenty years of big city living. Ever since his father took Christian under his wing fifteen years earlier, Trey had been something like an older brother to Christian. They'd always been able to talk. "Everything's fine at the paper," he said.

"Then it must be Gabriella Michaelson who's giving you fits."

In spite of his generally lousy mood, Christian laughed. "You don't miss much, do you?"

"A publisher in absentia can't afford to miss much."

"I suppose not." Trey seemed to be waiting for more information, so Christian admitted, "I've made a mistake or two in dealing with Gaby. She has a lot of pride." He rubbed the back of his neck and scowled. "That can make her a little prickly to be around."

Trey chuckled. "I remember my father using those very words to describe you, J.C.—when he got the bright idea to buy you a rusting hulk of a car, for instance. And when he offered you a staff reporting job on the *Journal* after you graduated from Tech. He was afraid you'd storm out in a huff."

"He did? When he gave me the job?" Christian was surprised to hear that. "By then I would have *begged* him to let me work for him. I owed your dad a lot."

"And you didn't resent his help?"

"Not by that time. I loved him. And I knew he loved me. That made the difference."

"So why don't you tell Gabriella you love her?"

Christian kept his brooding eyes on the road. "It's not that easy."

"I guess not, especially if you're still hung up on your own pride." Trey rolled down his window and took a deep breath of fresh air, staring out at the farmland as they neared Big Spring. He shook his head in wry amusement. "Well, old boy, for your sake I hope her career's about to take off. If it does, maybe she won't be quite so prickly about accepting help. Maybe she won't *need* any help. She really does the most remarkable work."

Christian shot his friend a quick, speculative look. Something in his tone of voice made Christian wonder if Trey Lang might be the anonymous donor who was going to commission Gaby. It would be totally within character. And it would certainly explain Trey's secretive, self-satisfied grin.

* * *

Gabriella was disappointed when she awoke to discover that Christian had gone without telling her goodbye. She dressed in a chambray prairie skirt, Western shirt and boots, then took her sketchpad and headed for Fort Concho. By the time the shops opened, she'd already roughed out an idea or two for her unknown benefactor.

Maxine Presswell came in to see her while Louise and Jack were browsing in Gabriella's building, and Gaby left Louise watching her table and went to have coffee with Miss Presswell at the saloon.

"I'd like very much to represent you," the older woman said frankly. "Quite a few of my contacts are looking for Southwestern art. And I can see from the pieces displayed here that you have the potential to branch out. The pirate is one of the most intriguing things I've ever seen."

They talked for nearly an hour, discussing contract terms and Gaby's previous bitter experience with an agent. "I can understand your hesitance, but I want to leave this contract with you so you can look over it. Feel free to consult with an attorney. And do be sure and check with some of my current clients to see if they're satisfied." Miss Presswell smiled with dry humor. "I can assure you, I don't usually have to beg artists to let me handle their work."

Gaby walked back to her booth rather dejectedly, wondering what it would take to get Christian to read the contract. After what he'd said to her last night, she didn't think she'd better mention the word *sculpture* to him.

By four o'clock, she'd actually sold a bronze and had dreamed up several more ideas for Bob Turnbow's donor, although she'd been too busy to put them down on paper. Bitsy had just returned from an early supper and was encouraging Gaby to go eat when Mrs. Conklin rushed in looking worried. "Gabriella, I need to locate John Christian. Do you know where he is?"

"He's out of town on business. What's the matter?"

"The switchboard operator has an urgent message for him. Someone in Kerrville has been trying to get in touch to tell him his father's been taken to the hospital. John Christian needs to get there as quickly as possible. It appears to be very serious."

Fourteen

———

The image that came to Gabriella frightened her. Suddenly, very clearly, she pictured Christian's father in distress...old, frail and weakened by his heart condition. Christian had tried to take care of him, but now, when John Lindsey was sick, Christian was out of town.

She would have to do what she could to help. Christian probably wouldn't make it back to San Angelo for several more hours, and her heart ached at the thought of Mr. Lindsey all alone in a hospital, possibly dying.

Gabriella forgot everything else. Bitsy and Mrs. Conklin assured her they would see that her sculpture was taken care of, but if they hadn't been there she would have left just as hastily. Barely taking time to grab her purse, she ran for her car. She was halfway to Kerrville before she remembered the agent's contract and her sketchpad of proposals. The Lord only knew where she had left them. Gaby certainly couldn't spare the time to worry about them.

When she finally arrived at the hospital and was directed to John Lindsey's room, she encountered several of his friends in the hall that she'd met at his church on Thanksgiving. "How is Mr. Lindsey?" she asked anxiously.

One of them, a middle-aged woman, gave Gabriella's arm a soothing pat. "He seems a little improved. We thought at first he'd had another heart attack, but the doctor says he hasn't."

Gaby learned that after being unable to reach him on the telephone, his friends had gone out searching for John Lindsey and had found him around noon, unconscious beside the road. They surmised that John had spent several days taking care of a needy family who were all sick with the flu and that he was trying to walk back home when he collapsed. Apparently he was suffering from a combination of the flu and exhaustion. "It's not as serious as we thought when we called," the kind-faced woman said. "Still, he's been asking for his son. Is John Christian coming?"

"He should be on his way by now. I'll wait here so you all can go home." She shook hands gratefully with each of them. "Thank you very much for everything you've done."

When they'd gone, she tiptoed into the room and found John Lindsey asleep, looking more otherworldly than ever. She sat down beside his bed and began praying that he wouldn't die.

The nurses checked him every so often, and the doctor came in and listened to his heart without disturbing the old man's sleep. Some time later he stirred and opened his eyes to look around vaguely. Gaby stood up so he could see her smiling down at him. Before she could ask if he needed anything, he closed his eyes again, a tiny smile on his lips.

She talked to him then, quietly telling him that he had to get well, if not for his own sake, then for Christian's. "He loves you, you know, and that makes you lucky." Her voice grew husky. "You've done a fine job of raising your son, Mr. Lindsey. I admire him more than anyone I've ever known." In a whisper she added, "I love him so much!"

Outside, the December night darkened. Gaby must have dozed off, because the sound of footsteps on the bare floor jerked her back to full consciousness. Sitting up, she saw Christian approach the bed, a darkly handsome pirate in a navy-blue business suit, minus the necktie, his top shirt buttons undone. He glanced at her with unfathomable eyes, then went directly to the sleeping patient. "Pop," he said gruffly. "Pop, I'm here."

Gaby felt tears prick her eyes, but whether they were caused by compassion or relief or weariness, she didn't know. She got to her feet and slipped out of the room, and after a while Christian came out. Not sparing her a greeting, he spoke shortly. "Have you seen the doctor?"

"I think he's at the nurses' station." His terseness puzzled her. She told herself as she watched him stride down the hall that he was just tired and worried about his father. He had started limping, so it must have been a bad day for him.

There was a remote look in his eyes when he came back. Icy fingers of fear clutched at her heart as they faced each other in the empty hallway. "Did the doctor have bad news for you?"

Frowning, he reached up to rub one hand down the back of his neck. "Not really. He thinks Dad's going to be okay, although he's pretty weak."

Joyous relief and tenderness surged through her and brought more tears, enough this time to fill her eyes. She reached for him and began to sob, too tired to hold back her emotions. Thank God Mr. Lindsey wouldn't die!

"Gaby—" He broke off impatiently, gritting his teeth. He'd been so damned worried as he drove from San Angelo—afraid for his father, but also for Gaby, who report-

edly had driven off from Fort Concho like a maniac. He'd
half expected to find her Chevy wrapped around a tree
somewhere along the way, and the sight of it parked innoc-
uously in front of the hospital when he arrived had trig-
gered an unreasonable fury inside him in spite of his relief.
Knowing her independence, he figured she probably would
have told him not to worry about her . . . to mind his own
business. As if he could turn his concern off and on to please
her!

Christian's muscles were wound up so tight they literally
hurt, and for once having her arms around him only made
the tension more difficult to bear. It took a tremendous effort just to keep his voice level. "Gaby, what are you crying
about?"

"I was so scared!" she confessed, unconsciously echoing
his own feelings. "I was afraid he was going to die, and I
didn't know how I could help you if he didn't make it."

"You wanted to help me?"

She didn't notice the frost in his tone. Tightening her
arms, she clung to him, absorbing the staccato pounding of
his heart against her cheek, thinking how very much she
loved him. "Oh, God, Christian, I didn't want you to be
hurt! If I could hold you forever and protect you, I would.
Life has hurt you enough."

She felt him grow very still before he pushed her away
from him. "You think so, Gaby?" Held at arm's length, she
couldn't help seeing that his shirt was a mess from her tears,
his face a rigid mask. Distracted, she wiped her damp cheeks
and sniffled, finally recognizing his anger. He didn't even try
to disguise it when he said harshly, "You think the fact that
I only have one leg ought to exempt me from any more
problems?"

"I . . . not exactly." The fire snapping in his hazel eyes
confused her. What was he so mad about? Was his rage left

over from last night, when she'd mistakenly thought he might be the anonymous donor? She swallowed. "Whether you have one leg or ten, I wouldn't want anything bad to happen to you, Christian." A million more wretched tears seemed to be welling up in her eyes, and she blinked and tried to force them away. It didn't work; they spilled over in an embarrassing flood. "I worry about your working too hard and staying on your feet too long and maybe giving away your last dime to help someone else—like your father, because you *are* like him, whether you know it or not."

"Is that right?" Christian felt the anger explode inside him, contaminating every cell of his body. He was shaking with it, wondering how she dared to think it was all right for her to cry over him when she wouldn't grant him the same privilege. "Well, Gabriella, if that's the truth, there's not a damn thing you can do about it. Anyway, it's nothing for you to concern yourself about. I suggest that you don't give it another thought."

His grip on her upper arms was no more painful than the bitter lash of his words. She tried to pull away, protesting, "That's easier said than done."

"No kidding?" he muttered sarcastically. Did she think she'd ever made it easy for him? He released her, his expression grim. "Gaby, what in the name of all that's holy are you doing here? Why did you come?"

She rubbed her arms, feeling utterly bewildered. "Don't you know?"

"Because you were worried about me? Well, let me tell you something—the last thing in this world that I want is for you to worry about me. It wasn't a very good idea for you to come here." He turned toward the closed door of the hospital room. "I can take care of my father just fine, thank you."

Gaby's chest constricted, making it nearly impossible for her to breathe. She stared at Christian through a film of tears as he pushed open the door and disappeared inside his father's room, and the anguish built up in her throat with incredible force. She had to clench her jaws together to hold back the wail that would have announced to the entire floor of the hospital what had happened.

But what *had* happened? She didn't have the foggiest idea, except that Christian had made it very plain he didn't want her here. Well, that was one thing she could remedy.

Five minutes later she stood fumbling with her keys at the turquoise-and-white Chevrolet, finding it difficult to unlock the door. Despite the streetlight, she couldn't see a foot in front of her nose for the blasted tears. Damn him anyway! Life never used to be this complicated, she thought.

She'd just succeeded in opening the door when she heard a hoarse shout from the front entry of the hospital. "Gabriella Michaelson!" Christian roared. "Don't you dare get in that car!"

When she glanced across the lawn at him, then ignored the order and climbed in, he broke into an awkward run across the grass, stumbling and almost falling when he leaped over a low hedge and a flowerbed. Gaby sat transfixed, her fingers curled around the steering wheel as she watched his distinctly hobbled approach.

When he reached the car, he pressed his hands flat on the fender to support himself and bent over the hood, his chest heaving. Her heart in her throat, she cautiously got back out into the chilly evening and let the door swing shut. Was he all right? She didn't dare ask. Instead, she blurted, "That was stupid."

He lifted his dark head and glared at her. "*That* was stupid? What do you call running away from me?"

She corrected him with dignity. "I was leaving, which is what you wanted. You said I shouldn't have come."

Shaking his head, he hunched his broad shoulders and drew in several more deep breaths, then straightened up and turned toward her. In the semidarkness, his face looked strained. Gaby hated herself because she wanted to reach up and smooth away the tired lines etching his eyes and his mouth.

"You shouldn't have come—that's true," he was saying. "But turning right around and hightailing it back home won't solve anything. It's just as insane as coming down here in the first place. Just as dangerous, too, considering your mood. You'd probably wipe out on one of those hilly curves between here and San Angelo."

"I wouldn't think you'd care." Even as the words tumbled out, she knew it was a ridiculous thing to say. He might regret his involvement with her, but Christian was by far the most caring man she knew.

With lightning-quick speed, he grabbed her shoulders and held her still. From his taut expression, she thought he was debating what to do with her. Then abruptly he gathered her against him and wrapped her in his arms, holding her right against his thundering heart. "Lord, Gaby, you can't believe that!"

She inhaled his sexy scent and almost melted. He was infusing her with his warmth, confounding all her defenses. "You certainly haven't acted lately as if you care what becomes of me."

"Not care what becomes of you!" he groaned, weaving one hand into the thick length of her hair. He tugged her head back so he could stare straight into her eyes, letting her see the stomach-twisting despair in his. "If anything happened to you..." A shudder rippled through him. "It would kill me, Gaby. The thought of it tears me up inside."

Her eyes filled up—a permanent condition, it would seem. She figured she might as well stop fighting the tears and let them fall. "I appreciate your friendship, Christian," she said miserably. "I know I should be grateful for whatever scrap of affection you throw my way. But I've given this a lot of thought, and...the simple truth is, it would never be enough. I would always want more from you than you could give me."

His dark, slightly arching brows drew together. "What would you always want from me?"

She dropped her gaze to the mussed up front of his shirt, humiliated that she should have to spell it out. "Your love."

Not knowing whether to shake her or kiss her, he ended up leaning forward a couple of inches and feathering his mouth across her forehead. "And just exactly what," he said with tender exasperation, "do you think I've been trying to give you for the past month?"

Her head tipped back and her eyes jumped to meet his. "Sex?"

His lips quirked. "Besides that."

"Well...well, I don't know. You *did* tell me I shouldn't have come here today," she reminded him. "If you love me, why wouldn't you want me here?"

His smile vanished. "It's not that I didn't want you here, Gaby. For one thing, I was afraid you'd left your career in shambles back at Fort Concho. I'll bet you didn't leave any word for Maxine Presswell or Bob Turnbow, did you? Were your proposals ready for the anonymous benefactor?"

"No, but I don't care. If I get the commission, fine. If not, I'll survive. You once told me people have to matter more than things. Compared to your father, my sculpture doesn't matter at all." She lifted her chin. "But of course, you don't need my help to take care of your father, do you?"

His eyes fell away from hers for a moment, then he looked back up guiltily. "Gaby, that was a lie. I *do* need your help. I need you for a lot of things." He hesitated, then exhaled in a rush. "Would you come back inside so we can tell Dad good-night?"

There were plenty of questions Gabriella wanted to ask him, but she thought for the moment he'd said enough. A shy smile lit her face and she nodded.

Together they turned, Christian's arm across her shoulders and hers around his waist, and started for the hospital entrance. After limping a couple of steps, he chuckled. "I guess you were right—I wasn't cut out for the sprint team."

She grinned up at him. "Does this mean you don't plan to jump over the flower bed again?"

Wincing, he shook his head. "I've already done enough damage for one day."

She tightened her grip on him and wedged her shoulder beneath his. "I'm strong. You can lean on me."

His warm hazel eyes searched hers for a long moment before he nodded. "I had a feeling I probably could."

They both stayed with Mr. Lindsey until he settled down to sleep for the night. When they finally left the hospital, they drove to a nearby motel. Gabriella was determined to stay in Kerrville with Christian rather than return to San Angelo, and because Christian had figured out who the anonymous donor was, he didn't argue with her. Trey Lang, he knew, would wait for the proposal once he realized why Gaby had rushed out of town.

Gaby thought a long hot bath might help Christian's leg. Christian thought a bath with Gaby would do wonders for his entire body, not to mention his spirit. Despite the restrictions of the tub, they proved each other correct. She lay on top of him in the water as it cooled and trailed a lazy finger down the hard slope of his chest, admiring his taut muscles. "This is nice, isn't it?"

He had to stretch to plant a sultry kiss on the damp, dusky nipple that was poised above his mouth. "Mmm . . . yes, it certainly is!"

At the moist, throbbing touch of his kiss, a helpless shiver of need wrenched its way up through Gaby. Thinking she must be getting cold, Christian reached around her and moved the lever to open the drain. While the water level receded they both stood up and dried off, Gaby having a hard time keeping her thoughts calm. Then, wrapped only in a towel, Christian hopped agilely into the bedroom and stretched out on the bed with Gabriella following close behind him, unwilling to let him get farther away than arm's reach.

"Come here, angel," he whispered, one hand outstretched to her. "Let me warm you." When she curled up next to him without hesitation, he began to move his hands over her smooth flesh with growing ardor, drawing her close to him, slowly exploring her satin contours and molding her softness to his steel, spreading her legs and making himself at home between them.

When he filled her with his arousal, his heat began to flow into her as he'd known it would. He loved her with all his strength and gentleness, lifting her by gradual stages toward a summit of sublime awareness. Long after the first intensity had crested and then waned, wave after wave of sweet feeling continued to lap at the two of them, caressing, soothing, completely surrounding them.

By that time both were flushed and warm and thoroughly satisfied. "How're you doing?" he asked, a little out of breath.

She nuzzled his throat. "I've never been better!" The delicious sensations were still pulsing through her. "How does your leg feel?" One gentle hand massaged it for him.

"Terrific. I'll jump hurdles every day if you promise you'll personally handle my therapy." He lifted his head and gazed solemnly into her eyes. "Gaby, that's something else I need that only you can give me. Do you remember the night we first made love? Remember where you kissed me?"

"I kissed you everywhere you'd lie still for."

"You kissed my leg. That was the first time in fifteen years that I've felt completely whole—as if what I don't have doesn't matter." His expression was ineffably tender. "You don't think I could ever let you go after that, do you?"

His words revealed how truly vulnerable he'd been that night. Despite his courageous spirit, he'd worried that his handicap would somehow make him unworthy of her. And suddenly she understood that her own lifelong fear of failure, of not measuring up to her beautiful mother or her successful father, was as big a handicap as Christian's physical one. It was Christian and his warm acceptance of her that had given her the strength to overcome her fears.

"When you kissed the ugliest part of me," he was saying hoarsely, "I knew I had to persuade you to love me the way I love you."

Shaking her head, she said, "I've loved you from the very first, Christian...even when it began to seem that you didn't care any longer about me. Even when it got to the point that every time I tried to talk to you about my career, you changed the subject."

He sat up, a movement that untangled their arms and legs. When she caught his arm, muttering a quick, soft protest at the idea of his leaving her, he shook off her hand in a gesture that was clearly preoccupied. "Now wait a minute,

Michaelson! Don't you dare throw that in my face." Frustration etched a scowl on his darkly handsome face, but his eyes reflected deep pain. "In case you've forgotten, it was your brilliant idea that I shouldn't interfere with your career. I was only trying to play by your rules, which I hated, by the way. The last I heard, *you* wanted me to mind my own business."

For the first time, she understood how hard it had been on him when she so bluntly refused his help. Christian, she realized with a stunning blow of overdue insight, had long ago been forced to come to terms with his own weakness and needs. He'd faced the fact that his leg was gone, that he couldn't walk without his prosthesis. With remarkable grace he'd learned to yield his pride and accept help for the things he couldn't do by himself. In spite of all that, or maybe *because* of it, he was a man—what an incredible man!

And there was nothing—absolutely nothing at all—wrong with Gabriella accepting help from a fellow human being. Particularly from the man she loved. It was no admission of defeat. On the contrary, it was probably the first step in the right direction that she'd taken in a long time.

She spoke humbly. "I was a fool, Christian. It took me a while to see that I needed your help every bit as much as I wanted to help you." Drawing a shaky breath, she added, "But by then it seemed you'd really lost interest."

"I never lost interest for a minute!"

Gabriella wanted desperately to believe he meant what he was saying. "But, Christian—you acted as if—"

"That's just it, Gaby—I *acted*." Dropping backward and landing beside her with a soft bounce, he pillowed one arm beneath his head and looked at her wryly. "You'd told me a couple of hundred times that you could make it without me, so I tried to act the way I thought you wanted. But as for what *I* wanted—I wanted to have the right to pay your bills...to show off your sculpture to all my friends...to see that you met the best agent in the Southwest. In other words, I wanted to love you and share your whole life."

She lay on her side, staring at him, at the beloved face so close to her own. "Did you arrange for Maxine Presswell to come see my work at Fort Concho?"

His gaze didn't flicker from hers. "No. I talked to Miss Presswell about your work right after I met you. She gave me several ideas for promoting your career, none of which earned your approval when I attempted to put them into action. After hearing about your talent again from several other people, she decided to check out your pieces for herself. If she offered to represent you, I had nothing to do with it."

"She did," Gabriella said quietly, "and I think I'm going to take her up on it. I realize I'll never be able to market my own work adequately."

"Good for you! It's important to know your own limitations." He sat up again abruptly, his chin jutting. "This past month has taught me something about myself, too, Gaby. I'm not willing to settle for being just halfway involved with you. I want more than your nights and your free weekends. I want you as my wife, my equal partner, someone who can accept help as well as give it. So you'd better make up your mind: do you want me in your life or out of it?"

Prepared to argue, threaten, beg or cajole in order to win her to his side, he never got a chance. The instant the question was out of his mouth, Gaby scrambled onto his lap. She slid her hands behind his neck, and the dew-soft tips of her breasts teased his chest as she pressed longingly against him, giving him her answer without her saying a single word.

Breathing unsteadily, he pulled back just a bit to study her for a long, intent moment. "No doubts, Gabriella?" He reached up and fingered the tiny hole that marked his earlobe. "I'll always be different. Are you sure you can live with that?"

She gave him a soft, infinitely loving smile and touched her index finger to her lips, then to his pierced ear, their secret symbol for his uniqueness. "I'm sure I can't live without you. Even if I live to be a hundred, I'll never get enough of loving you."

He enveloped her swiftly, powerfully, in his arms. Just before he burrowed his dark face into her hair, she saw the sexy white smile transform it...saw his happiness infuse him with a radiance that stopped her heart for one long, glorious moment.

"Don't worry, Gaby," he said, his laughter warm against her throat. "We have all of eternity to work on that."

* * * * *

THE COMPELLING
AND UNFORGETTABLE SAGA OF
THE CALVERT FAMILY

April	August	November
£2.95	£3.50	£3.50

From the American Civil War to the outbreak of World
War I, this sweeping historical romance trilogy depicts
three generations of the formidable and captivating
Calvert women – Sarah, Elizabeth and Catherine.

The ravages of war, the continued divide of North and
South, success and failure, drive them all to discover an
inner strength which proves they are true Calverts.

Top author Maura Seger weaves passion, pride, ambition
and love into each story, to create a set of magnificent
and unforgettable novels.

W●RLDWIDE

FRUIT SALAD WORDSEARCH
COMPETITION!

How would you like a years supply of Silhouette Desire Romances ABSOLUTELY FREE? Well, you can win them! All you have to do is complete the word puzzle below and send it in to us by Dec. 31st. 1989. The first 5 correct entries picked out of the bag after that date will win **a years supply of Silhouette Desire Romances** (*six books every month - worth over £90*) What could be easier?

```
T E T A N A R G E M O P
A N E Y E P A R G A A E
N E A R S P I M N N T A
G N P R T L W E A D Y C
E I R E R E I L R A R H
R R I B A U K O O R R M
I A C P W R C N O I E A
N T O S B A R K E N H N
E C T A E E F R C U C A
I E T R R P O G N A M N
T N A R R U C D E R L A
E E H C Y L L E M O N B
```

RASPBERRY	**ORANGE**	**LYCHEE**
REDCURRANT	**MANGO**	**CHERRY**
BANANA	**LEMON**	**KIWI**
TANGERINE	**APRICOT**	**GRAPE**
STRAWBERRY	**PEACH**	**PEAR**
POMEGRANATE	**MANDARIN**	**APPLE**
BLACKCURRANT	**NECTARINE**	**MELON**

PLEASE TURN OVER FOR DETAILS ON HOW TO ENTER →

HOW TO ENTER

All the words listed overleaf, below the word puzzle, are hidden in the grid. You can find them by reading the letters forward, backwards, up or down, or diagonally. When you find a word, circle it or put a line through it, the remaining letters (which you can read from left to right, from the top of the puzzle through to the bottom) will spell a secret message.

After you have filled in all the words, don't forget to fill in your name and address in the space provided and pop this page in an envelope (you don't need a stamp) and post it today. Hurry - competition ends December 31st. 1989.

Silhouette Competition,
FREEPOST,
P.O. Box 236,
Croydon,
Surrey. CR9 9EL
Only one entry per household

Secret Message _____

_____

Name _____

Address _____

_____

_____ Postcode _____

You may be mailed as a result of entering this competition
Please tick the box if you are a Reader Service subscriber ☐

mps MAILING PREFERENCE SERVICE

SCOMP7